330265217

CW00432164

KI	WN	HE			
9/13	1/15	2/16			

FRAMLANDS
4/6/15

TL 2/17
JUNE 8/17
TL 3/18
TL 2/19

To renew this book, phone 0845 1202811 or visit
our website at www.libcat.oxfordshire.gov.uk
(for both options you will need your library PIN
number available from your library),
or contact any Oxfordshire library

 **OXFORDSHIRE**
COUNTY COUNCIL

L017-64 (01/13)

I'LL BE THERE

I'LL BE THERE

Deborah Grace Staley

CHIVERS

British Library Cataloguing in Publication Data available

This Large Print edition published by AudioGO Ltd, Bath, 2013.
Published by arrangement with Belle Books Inc.

U.K. Hardcover   ISBN   978 1 4713 2442 0
U.K. Softcover   ISBN   978 1 4713 2443 7

Printed and bound in Great Britain by T J International Ltd

DEDICATION

This is for Katy Zirbel,
a beautiful, intelligent,
strong, brave woman
who, just like the
heroines I love to create,
had the courage to write her own story.

WELCOME

"Hi, y'all. Welcome to Angel Ridge and what could be the worst winter on record here. Dixie Ferguson's the name, and I run Ferguson's, the finest eating establishment in town, if I do say so myself.

"You've chosen to visit us at an unusual time. Normally, I'd describe Angel Ridge as a sleepy little picturesque town that sits high on a ridge above Tellassee Lake, but things aren't always like they seem on the surface. Why, around here, the guy who wears overalls and no shirt in the summer is just as likely to be a millionaire as he is to be down on his luck. Take the newcomer who moved to town last fall. She wasn't at all like she seemed either. Why, she had family secrets even she didn't know about.

"Before I go into that, let me take a second to tell you a bit about the place I've called home for most of my life. Angel Ridge, population three hundred forty, is located in the valley of the Little Tennessee River and was established in 1785. In the early days, its first families — the McKays, the Wallaces, the Houstons, the Joneses, and the Craigs — staked their claims on hundreds of acres of the richest bottomland anyone had ever seen. They built big ol' homes near the meandering river and operated prosperous plantations. Well, all except for the Craigs. They were traders and craftsmen. Men of commerce, as it were. Meanwhile, the town developed above the river on a high ridge.

"In the early 1970's, the Flood Control Board came in and bought up most of the property along the flood prone river, and those stately homes that some called relics of a bygone era, were inundated in the name of progress. But those who built more modest Victorians near town up on the ridge? Well, their homes are still standin'. Of course, the families who lost theirs to the newly formed Tellassee Lake moved up to the ridge as well and built elaborate Victorian mansions such as this quaint little town had never seen.

"Most of the families I mentioned earlier are still around. These are hardy folks. Why, in all the time they've lived here, they've endured Indian attacks, floods, divided loyalties in the Civil War, and yes, even feuds. The older folks are still marked by the hardships of the past, but the young people of the town hope to move beyond old hurts to create a new generation made strong because of their roots, yet free of the past.

"As I said, last fall Candi Heart rented the old beauty shop across the way on Main Street and opened up a girly shop called, 'Heart's Desire' and along with it, a closet full of skeletons. Her shop's a fun place that sells a bit of everything a girl loves: flowers, candy, lingerie, clothing, perfumes and lotions. Why, she even serves tea in the back. It's a nice place where girls can get together and talk. I just love the place and Candi, but she had no idea that her coming here would rattle some old, rusty chains. Yes, trouble followed that girl to town and Jenny Thompson, who runs our newspaper, *The Angel Ridge Chronicle,* got tangled up in the mess.

"I've lived here most of my life, and I can't remember ever locking my doors at night, but I confess to locking up now and checking them again before I go to bed. I've even caught myself looking over my shoulder as I walk down Main for anyone that might seem suspicious. I hate feeling this way. I never thought things in Angel Ridge would come to this, but that just goes to show you that every town, even a picture-postcard one, has its troubles.

"Not much goes on around here in the winter. After Christmas, folks usually hunker down and wait for spring to come. Given recent events, I'd say people in town are understandably on edge. I guess you could say that's where our heroine, Jenny Thompson, and hero, Cord Goins, are — on edge, hunkered down and waiting. After an explosion at the newspaper, everyone assumed that Jenny had met her untimely demise. I'm ashamed to admit that I've even helped promote the deception. I really had no other choice.

"Now Jenny and Cord are stuck between a beginning and an ending, and both of them powerless to control the situations they've found themselves in. But that's when a person can also find themselves in uncharted territory just waiting to venture out and make their own way. I've got a feeling Jenny and Cord will find their way.

"So keep safe and warm during your visit to Angel Ridge, and if you have time, come by the diner and have yourself a cup of hot chocolate on me."

PROLOGUE

Jenny Thompson stood outside the door to Ferguson's Diner, looking in. She knocked on the locked door without much hope that anyone would be inside. Nearly every citizen of Angel Ridge would be at church on a Sunday morning; everyone but her. She'd been up all night working on an investigative report blowing the top off the crime ring behind the recent break-ins that had occurred in Angel Ridge.

Dixie Ferguson emerged from the kitchen, giving her a wave, then came and unlocked the door. "Jenny! Get yourself in here, girl!"

Jenny smiled and walked into the warm, inviting old-fashioned diner complete with checkerboard tile, green vinyl booths, and a lunch counter. "I'm surprised to see you, Dixie. I thought you'd be in church."

"And yet you're here knocking on my door."

"I had a craving for chocolate ice cream."

"Never let a good lunch get between a woman and her chocolate."

Jenny laughed. "Everything okay, Dixie? You look tired."

Dixie picked up a mug and sipped her coffee. "I could say the same about you, not that you don't cover it well with that fabulous pantsuit." She held up her cup. "Can I get you some?"

"Yes, thanks." She could use a break and the chat with a good friend.

"Susan had a rough night," Dixie said as she poured.

The mayor's wife, Susan Houston, was Dixie's best friend. She'd just been diagnosed with breast cancer. "I'm sorry to hear that Susan's not doing well."

Dixie sat at the stool next to Jenny's. "I know they say what doesn't kill you makes you stronger, but I'm not so sure. The chemo is brutal."

They both drank their coffee in silence for a moment. How could something so awful happen to such a young, vital woman with children to raise?

"So what are you blaming your restless night on?"

"Work."

Dixie shook her head and, amused, Jenny couldn't help noticing her friend's hair which was short, spiked and some shade of red not found in nature, but on Dixie, it worked.

"You know what they say, all work and no play . . ."

"I know, but I found out a long time ago that I don't have time for the games men play. Anything beyond a couple of dates and they start giving you hell about working too much, but when they work too much, that's a different matter all together. I don't need anyone trying to run my life but me."

Dixie held up her coffee cup in a salute. "Amen to that, but it does get lonely."

"I wouldn't know. Too busy," Jenny joked, but the old familiar ache in the region of her heart called her a liar.

"You have to go to bed sometime and not that I'd know, but I hear there's something to be said for a long, warm, hard body to snuggle up to."

Jenny fell into what she did best — putting up a wall with humor. She smiled. "Do tell . . ." and sipped her coffee.

Dixie sighed. "I would like to try it once, just to say I did."

"Have someone in mind?"

"I wish."

The two friends laughed. "So, you must be on the trail of a hot story." Dixie commented.

"*Mmm,*" Jenny nodded.

Dixie clapped and rubbed her hands together. "I love a good exposé. Tell me."

Jenny thought about that for a minute. There were certain aspects of the story that were out there for anyone to find if they cared to dig. Other information, however, she would turn over to the authorities. A lot of people were going to prison because of what she'd found. "Turns out that Candi's mother lived here twenty-some years ago. Came down from the mountain, pretty as a picture, and had every man in town with a heartbeat falling at her feet, single and married alike."

Dixie's eyebrows rose. "I'm listening."

"You can imagine how the little church ladies in town felt about her."

"*Mmm-hmm.*"

"Unable to find a job here, she resorted to working at a gentleman's club in Vonore."

"A what?" Dixie exclaimed.

"A private club, tucked away out on some dirt road, where there was all manner of illegal activity going on."

"Such as?"

"Gambling, drinking, loan sharking, drugs, you name it. Oh, and exotic dancers just to add a little spice."

14

"Hold on." Dixie held up a hand and sat straighter. "Are you saying that sweet little Candi Heart's momma was an exotic dancer?"

"Well, let's just say she was a scantily clad *performer* who sang and did a passable imitation of Marilyn Monroe."

"And the men in Angel Ridge . . ."

"Had front row seats."

"Scandalous!"

"Indeed, that is until Candi's momma turned up dead, floating in a back water cove just outside of town."

"You mean murdered?" Dixie exclaimed.

"Well, officially she drowned, but given the kind she was involved with, I'm inclined to speculate."

"So what happened to these criminals running the place? Are they still around? Is that who's been causing trouble for Candi?"

"I suspect so. The club closed not long after Candi's momma died, but you know how these organizations work. There had to be someone on the outside with money paying these locals involved to run the operation. My guess is that some of them are still around and working at it under the table. Who knows, could be some of the businesses here in town are fronts for illegal activity."

15

"No way."

Jenny shrugged. After she published her piece, she'd turn it all over to the attorney general's office in Knoxville and let them sort it all out. She should probably get out of town for a few days. She'd been missing her sister, Frannie. Maybe she'd pay her a visit.

"Well, I need to get going." She stood and lifted her purse to her shoulder.

"Let me get you that ice cream."

"Thanks."

Dixie fixed her treat and handed it over. Jenny juggled to get her wallet out of her purse.

"Stop now. It's on me. Let me get the door for you."

"Thanks," Jenny said.

As she walked down the sidewalk back toward *The Chronicle,* she swirled her tongue along the point where her ice cream cone met the creamy chocolate that crowned it. Sweets were her weakness, chocolate in particular, in any form. She'd earned the treat after the all-nighter she'd pulled at the paper, not that she needed an excuse. She was a firm believer in living by her own terms, and that meant she had chocolate if she wanted chocolate — no guilt.

The sidewalks were deserted with everyone still in church, but services would be over soon. Jenny pushed her sunglasses up on her head as she stepped out of the warm autumn sunshine into the darkened alley that ran parallel to Main Street, the only major thoroughfare in downtown Angel Ridge. This side of the street housed *The Angel Ridge Chronicle* and the older businesses in town, such as Wallace's Grocery, McKay Bank and Trust, and the Apothecary Shoppe. The slower pace of the quaint little East Tennessee town had appealed to her when she'd moved here three years ago after living in Nashville where she'd worked as an investigative reporter at *The Tennessean.*

She rotated the cone as she swiped her tongue across the chocolaty treat. It had taken her all of a month to get bored.

She'd managed, but she had to admit she'd missed the thrill of breaking big stories. Thanks to Candi Heart, she'd gotten her feet wet again. Given what she'd found, she wondered if she'd been crazy to get involved, but only for a half second. Reveal the truth, and the rest will work itself out — that was her journalistic credo. She hoped that held true for the crime ring she'd uncovered, but seasoned instincts told her that an organization this established and this large wouldn't go down swiftly or quietly. It's the reason she hadn't hit "send" on the email that would place the story on the wire nationwide by morning. She wanted to proof it once more and have a little more time to think. This was a life-changing story; the biggest she'd ever had.

She shook her head and bit into the cone. Three years in this town and she'd gone soft. She'd send the story as soon as she got back to her desk.

She'd just tossed the rest of her cone into a garbage can when an explosion rocked the shops lining the alley. Jenny lost her balance and fell. Covering her head, she crawled behind the garbage can as a shower of shrapnel rained down.

When the ground stopped shaking and debris quit falling from the sky, Jenny chanced a look around her. Her winter white Donna Karan pantsuit was ruined, her Manolo Blahniks were missing a heel, and her ears were ringing. Other than that, she was fine, though her heart beat so hard and fast, she felt like it would burst.

She managed to stand on her broken shoes and walked between the buildings toward Town Square. Good Lord Almighty, it looked like a war zone. People spilling out of the two churches on either end of Main Street were shouting and running in all directions. A man crouched next to an unconscious woman while others knelt in the grass holding their heads. She heard Dixie say, "What happened?" and someone answer, "There's been an explosion at the newspaper."

She wobbled on her damaged pumps, ready to run out to confirm or refute what she'd just heard when something stopped her — something that froze in her gut and had her easing back into the shelter of the alley. *Someone had blown up the newspaper.*

Bud DeFoe, who ran the hardware, said, "First they break into Candi Heart's new shop, and then not two days later, they blow up our newspaper!"

"Where's Jenny?" she heard Dixie say.

"Do you think she was inside?"

"I don't know. She was just with me at the diner, but she's had time to get back to the paper. Oh Lord —"

"Why would someone want to blow up the newspaper?" Bud asked.

Why indeed? She'd been made. The long inactive crime syndicate that Candi Heart's arrival in town had stirred up meant to keep her from publishing her exposé. They'd destroyed her newspaper thinking her inside to shut her up — permanently. She retreated back into the alley completely, then made

19

her way quickly to the sheriff's office, thankfully unnoticed, what with all the commotion of people running in all directions and emergency personnel arriving.

As soon as she entered the back of the courthouse, she walked through the deserted rear offices straight to the jailhouse, which, as usual, was also empty. She pulled the heavy metal door closed that separated it from the front offices, slid to the floor and dug in her pocket for her phone. Jenny dialed the sheriff's personal cell number.

Grady Wallace had been sheriff in Angel Ridge since long before she'd bought the paper. She wouldn't call him a close personal friend. The best relationship she could hope for between the press and local law enforcement was cordial, and he was at least that — most of the time. He'd even agreed to work with her on this investigation, but she felt sure that was because he was more than a little interested in Candi.

There'd been a time when Jenny had thought that perhaps he might be attracted to her. As she'd told Dixie, she was not interested in a relationship, and certainly not with an officer of the law. Turns out he'd been powerless to resist this woman of mystery who had them all neck deep in this trouble.

"Wallace."

"Grady? It's Jenny Thompson."

"Jenny? Thank God you're all right! What the hell's going on? Woody just called and said there was an explosion at the newspaper."

"Well, that seems to be the consensus. I didn't stick around to investigate. Aren't you in town?"

"I was on the riverbank with Doc Prescott. I'm on my way back. Where are you?"

"Hiding out at the jail."

"Good call. I'll be there soon."

The call disconnected. Jenny sat on the floor, cross-legged, and waited. What should she do next? Jenny stood when she heard the handle turning in the metal door and saw Dixie's face framed in its small window.

"Thank God you're all right. I came over to get Grady, but when I looked back here, I saw you crouched on the floor. Are you okay?"

"I'm fine, but my shoes are ruined."

Dixie looked at the missing heel on her pump. "Well that is a shame," she commiserated, "but thank goodness you're all right. Were you inside the paper when the explosion happened?"

"No. I hadn't made it back yet."

"Well thank the Lord for that. Where's

Grady?"

"On his way. He was fishing."

"Just like a man to never be around when you need him. Here," she took Jenny's hand and helped her to a side door that led to a room with a table and several chairs. "You need to sit. You've had a shock. Can I get you anything?"

Jenny shook her head, but then took Dixie's hand. "Yes. Would you stay?"

Dixie sat immediately and squeezed Jenny's hand with both of hers. "Of course." After a moment had passed, Dixie asked, "Do you think this has something to do with that investigation you were telling me about?"

Jenny's heart sank. She'd been thinking the same thing, but hadn't wanted to put words to the thoughts. So, she just nodded.

Dixie put a hand to her mouth, her eyes wide as she considered the possible implications. Jenny wanted to laugh. She'd never seen Dixie speechless. It had to be a first.

"How can you sit there and smile like that? This is awful. Just awful!" Dixie said.

Oh well. It lasted all of about ten seconds before she found her tongue again. "I was just thinking I'd never known you to run out of something to say."

"You're right about that, hon, but this is a

unique situation, to say the least."

"Jenny?"

"In here, Grady," Dixie said, standing.

"You okay?" Grady asked as he rushed into the room. His glance slid over Jenny, as if checking her for signs of injury.

She figured a smart-ass reply along the lines of the one she'd given Dixie was in order, so she said, "My pantsuit is ruined."

Grady chuckled. "I'd say that's the least of your worries about now."

Dixie and Jenny exchanged a look.

"Men just don't get it," Dixie said.

"What are you doing here, Dix?"

"Looking for you," she said pointedly with a hand on her hip.

"You can't expect me to have known what was going to happen when I left to go fishing this morning."

"If you'd been in church where you should have been, you would have at least been close by when the town needed you."

Ignoring that, he turned to Jenny and asked, "What happened?"

"You know as much as I do. There was an explosion at the newspaper."

"Were you there?"

"No. I mean, I was there all night and part of the morning, but I had stepped out to go to the diner."

"Did you notice any suspicious activity, anyone in town who didn't belong?"

"No. Nothing."

He pushed her hair back. "There's blood coming out of your ear."

Jenny touched the spot and looked at the blood on her fingers. "Must have ruptured an eardrum. I was in the alley when the explosion happened."

"We'll get Doc Prescott to look at you." He rubbed the small scar on his chin. "Guess you stirred up a hornet's nest."

"I knew the risks when I started this. Your butt's on the line, too, you know."

"Comes with the badge. You know you can't go back into town."

Jenny nodded. "That's why I came here."

"What are you going to do?" Dixie asked Grady.

"I called the Tennessee Bureau of Investigation Office in Knoxville. They're on their way."

"What do they know?" Jenny asked.

"Everything. I called them after we talked yesterday, so they know what we're dealing with here."

"I don't like the sound of this," Dixie said.

Neither did Jenny. She ran a hand through her hair, letting it all sink in.

"Had you gone to print with your story?"

"No. It would have already been out on the wire for distribution at midnight if I hadn't wanted to proof it one more time."

"It's probably not a bad thing. I guess it's lost now."

Jenny didn't comment. She may have lost the paper, but she backed all her files up on a USB drive she carried in her purse, and she also uploaded a copy of everything to a dummy email file account on the Internet. She wasn't about to risk everything to see every last one of the criminals responsible go scot-free. She turned, frowning. Where was her purse? Damn it.

"What's wrong?" Grady asked.

"I lost my purse in the alley after the explosion."

"I'll radio Woody and ask him to get it," he offered. "After the TBI gets here, I'll have to get back to the . . ."

His words trailed off. Right. How did one put words to something like this? Jenny had spent most of her adult life reporting scenes and incidents like this, but never would she have thought she'd have to ascribe meaning to something so horrific, so unspeakable, to her own life.

Their eyes met, and Grady surprised Jenny by reaching out to squeeze her shoulder. "You did the right thing, Jenny."

She nodded and drew in a shaky breath. "I know."

They both knew what this meant. Years of training and familiarity with police procedure made it clear. She'd delved wholeheartedly into what had started as just another mystery to solve, a story to expose to the light of truth. But this time, there could be a heavy price to pay. Her freedom.

"Dixie, can you stay with her while I go attempt to establish some semblance of order and secure the crime scene?"

"Of course. Go."

Sometime later, the TBI officers arrived. They swore Dixie to silence and informed Jenny of what would happen now. She watched and listened like an observer hovering above the scene.

Ms. Thompson, thank you for your service to your community. Because of your sacrifice, a crime syndicate that has operated in the south for more than fifty years trafficking prostitutes, drugs, liquor, and stolen goods will be eliminated.

If you so choose, the U.S. Marshal Service will take your application for admittance into the Federal Witness Security Program. While your application is being processed, you will be taken into protective custody. The explosion was really a Godsend. People will as-

sume you were there. When you don't show up in town, they'll also assume you died in the explosion. In the interim, we'll get you to a temporary safe house. After you testify, you'll be relocated to a permanent location and given a new identity.

Jenny Thompson will cease to exist.

CHAPTER 1

Jenny lay on the stiff cot staring up in the direction of the rough-hewn ceiling. What she wouldn't give for her pillow top mattress and a pile of down-filled comforters. Her idea of roughing it was the Super 8, and this cabin, miles from civilization on some no-name mountain, was just a step up from sleeping in a tent. The cold, early January wind whistled through the cracks in the wood slats that doubled for walls. The thin military-style blanket provided only meager warmth.

It had been two months since she'd been taken into "protective" custody. In that time, she'd been moved from location to location. Each time because men with guns had found where they'd tucked her away. It was like they'd planted a sub-dermal tracking device on her.

She rolled to her side and stared out the break where the curtains didn't meet. Nothing but darkness. She loved it when stars dotted the sky. She never knew that being in the middle of nowhere with no artificial light for competition allowed for viewing them as nature intended. She'd noticed that during her many sleepless nights. Nighttime was often filled with activity, so that was when she did her thinking, since there was precious little else to do.

She wondered what was going on at home. Wondered how her sister was since she'd been told that Jenny had been placed in the witness protection program. She and her parents had never been close, but she truly missed her baby sister. Their mother's main concern had been to raise her and her sister as two proper southern ladies. Jenny had never fit that mold, not that she had tried. With their father pursuing a career in politics, he'd been mostly absent and happy to leave the childrearing to his wife.

The one constant had been that she and Frannie had had each other. At night after the ballet performances Daddy had missed, again, they'd cuddle under the covers and dry each other's tears. Jenny wrapped her arms around her midsection and squeezed, wishing that it was her sister's comforting arms around her. Could anything ever fill this ache inside her? She couldn't imagine never seeing Frannie again. Who had dried her sister's tears when some faceless voice on a phone had told her she'd never see or speak to Jenny again?

Gunfire rocked the cabin, shattering the stillness of the night. Jenny rolled off her bed onto the floor just before the window over the cot became a shower of glass.

A man entered the room, a gun poised in his hand. "Come with me," he ordered, before roughly hauling her to her feet. "Keep your head down." Jenny's breath came out in a rush when she saw that he was one of the U.S. Marshals guarding her.

The ancient timbers of the tiny, old cabin vibrated with the impact of a barrage of bullets. She ought to be frightened, but instead she was good and pissed. "What the hell happened? We're on the side of a godforsaken mountain. How do they keep finding us?"

The man beside her didn't respond. Instead, he shoved a moldy rug out of the way. Dust flew in all directions burning her eyes. He flung back a door in the floor revealing a gaping hole. Cool, musty air filtered up offering an invitation she would be unable to refuse.

"Get in."

Another marshal appeared in the doorway.

"I need you, Pierce. I can't hold them off on my own."

Pierce grasped her shoulders and looked into her eyes. "We talked about this when we got here. This tunnel is the only way out now." He shoved a flashlight at her and urged her down into the hole.

"How am I supposed to find some cave in the dark?"

"Go."

The rough-hewn door slammed shut and darkness surrounded her. She crouched just inside the tunnel, listening to the sounds above. The scratching of the rug being replaced, retreating footsteps, and finally the crash of a door breaking away from its frame. Then more gunfire. She clicked on the light, let instinct kick in and moved.

Slimy rocks lined the narrow, frozen path making footing treacherous. The low earthen ceiling required her to move in a crouched position. Cobwebs clung to her face and clothing. She gulped great breaths of the moist, stagnant air, but couldn't force enough into her lungs.

After weeks of changing locations in the middle of the night, she had learned to sleep prepared to run. Tonight she'd chosen sweatpants and a t-shirt with a sweatshirt tied at her waist. She'd worn shoes to bed for weeks now. She turned a corner and a rat scurried across the toe of her sneakers. A scream rose up in the back of her throat, but she pushed it down and kept moving.

The passage narrowed and ended. Jenny searched for a way out, but couldn't find one. *Perfect,* she thought. *I'm trapped in a cold, dark hole.* No marshals, no assassins, just rats that can eat away her flesh while she starved. Nice.

She closed her eyes and tried to breathe normally. *Get hold of yourself and think.* When she opened her eyes, she saw a makeshift door above her. She pushed against it, splinters bit into her palms, but nothing happened. She pushed harder, ignoring the pain, but it wouldn't budge. Squatting, she sprang upward, getting nothing but a bruised shoulder for her efforts. She surged up again, the wood tearing her thick cotton shirt. The door moved a little, so she repeated the process until she was able to wedge it open a few inches. She pushed and shoved until, finally, she had clawed her way out onto the leaf-strewn forest floor.

Standing, Jenny jumped on the door until it closed. She covered it with tree limbs and brush. And then she ran. She couldn't tell where she was going, but she had to put distance between her and the cabin. Hiding was her only objective. Her logical mind intruded telling her that if the assassins couldn't find her, would the marshals be able to? Her mind churned, but survival demanded cover. She'd worry about the rest later.

It was pitch-black tonight. The moist smell of rain or snow hung heavy in the air. She hoped to find the cave they'd scouted earlier before it came. Small tree branches bent against her progress and slapped her in the face. Tree roots tripped her, but she maintained her footing and kept going. Thank God for yoga that improved her flexibility and balance. She untied her sweatshirt from her waist and pulled it on as she jogged up the mountain, shining the flashlight in all directions searching. Forget the cave. Anything would do; a ditch, a rock —

She ran headlong into something solid. The force of the impact nearly knocked the breath from her. As she struggled to regain her footing, she realized that two strong hands held her upright. She pointed the flashlight at his face. She thought he looked familiar, but couldn't be sure. He was tall, dark, bearded. His pack declared him a hiker, but could she be sure? What if he was one of them?

"What the hell?" he mumbled.

He seemed as surprised as her, but she wasn't about to stand around and find out that he was about to murder her. If he thought Violet Jennings Thompson was going out without a fight, he was in for the shock of his life. All the anger and the months of hiding and having her life stolen from her by faceless men, who were less than scum, converged into blind fury. Adrenaline surged through her, and she pummeled and kicked, mindless in her rage. When he suddenly released her, she fell hard.

"Calm down, I'm not going to hurt you." He grabbed her flashlight and pointed it at her face. Blinded, she closed her eyes against the pain. "You," he murmured. "I thought you were dead."

Jenny heard people thrashing their way up the mountain. She scooted away, gaining her feet. Just a few more steps and she could disappear into the dense forest. He surged forward, gripping her arm it in a vise she couldn't escape, but she struggled anyway.

"Who's following you?"

Instinct told her to answer him honestly. "I'm not sure. Either marshals or —"

The man slung her over his shoulder and ran. "Hey!" She kicked, squirmed, and pounded his back with each labored step he took.

"Be still or I'll drop you on your head so you can break your neck," he growled.

She grabbed his coat with both hands and bided her time, vowing to renew her struggles as soon as her feet touched the ground.

Within moments, he ducked into a cave and dumped her onto the cold, hard ground. Numb with fear and cold, she didn't feel a thing. She couldn't be sure if he'd brought her to the same cave she and the marshals had scouted earlier. What if he'd been lying in wait for her? What if the plan had been for his fellow thugs to force her up the mountain where he'd grab her — hide her until they could catch up?

He went back outside and pulled several tree branches across the opening to the cave, confusing the scenario. Jenny's instincts told her to run, but the darkness inside the cave was so complete, she froze with indecision. When he'd finished, he used the flashlight to find his way back to her.

"What are you going to do to me?" Jenny demanded.

He shut off the light and whispered. "Unless you're sure those are marshals out there, you might want to keep quiet."

"How do I know you're not one of the ones who are after me?"

"If I wanted to kill you, why would I hide you?"

Why indeed. She could hear her pursuers nearing and her anxiety grew. She couldn't be sure of anything. What if she was right and this was a plan? That they knew where he'd hidden her? So, she decided to reason with him.

"You'll spend the rest of your life in jail if you kill me," she said. "It's not too late for you to do the right thing. Let me go, and I swear I won't tell anyone about you."

The man leaned in close to her. She could feel his heat, could sense his intensity. Near her ear he spoke evenly, "You're safe."

An inappropriate fission of awareness skidded up her spine, while outside, twigs snapped, leaves rustled, muffled voices grew louder. Then, something unbelievable happened. The sounds receded and stillness settled around them. Trembling and weak with relief, Jenny rested her head against knees she'd pulled up to her chest and thanked God.

Jenny jumped when she heard the man beside her move. She'd almost forgotten she wasn't alone.

He pressed something soft against her

36

legs. "Here. It's cold and you don't have a coat."

"I'm fine."

"Take it. It'll get colder before morning."

The concern lacing his words started another of those inappropriate shivers. His deep, slow southern drawl sounded so familiar. Like the accents of the people from the mountain communities who came into Angel Ridge to shop on weekends.

"Who are you?"

No response. No movement. Just his even breathing and hers, which was much more labored.

"Do I know you?"

Still nothing.

"You said you thought I was dead. Why?"

"We best keep quiet. They might still be nearby." He took the coat and leaned even closer. Reaching out a hand, he fumbled until he found her shoulder, then draped the coat around her. Squeezing her arm, he said, "Try to rest. I'll scout the area first light to see if it's safe to leave."

He withdrew far enough away that she could no longer feel his warmth, and Jenny felt inexplicably alone.

She'd hoped to find a safe haven. She never imagined she'd share shelter with a stranger. He was right. If he'd wanted to harm her, he could have done it already. Still, she'd stay alert and wait till morning when she'd have light and could look in his eyes. She'd made a career of trusting her instincts. They would tell her what to do.

A sound at the entrance to the cave startled them both. Her protector groped in the darkness for something. Someone moved rapidly towards them. There was a metallic clicking and then the piercing brightness of the flashlight lit the cave. Jenny blinked and a squirrel came into focus. Both man and animal stared at each other in fear for a moment. Then the rodent scurried off, retracing its steps to the forest.

The man collapsed against the wall of the cave, his breath coming in quick, shallow gasps. Propping his elbows on bent knees, he blocked his eyes with the barrel of the flashlight and rubbed his forehead with the back of his hand.

Jenny's breath came out in a whoosh of air.

The man jumped and pointed a gun at her, then remembering, lowered it, releasing the hammer. He must have forgotten she was there. Her body tingled as his eyes traveled the length of her body. He looked away, but Jenny searched features only partially revealed by the beam of the flashlight, surprised by the stark beauty the half-light could not mask. Dark skin, silky, long black hair and beard, mysterious eyes that refused to meet hers.

The flip of a switch on the flashlight submerged them once again in total darkness. Jenny heard him inhale deeply. "I'll keep watch. It's only a few hours to sunrise."

She had to be careful what she told him. He had protected her from immediate danger, but she had to focus on the fact that she really knew nothing about him. Pushing loose hair back towards her ponytail, she shook off the languid feelings still muddling her brain.

Weigh the facts . . . He has a gun. He could have killed you, but he didn't. He'd protected her. She would trust him for now, but as soon as opportunity presented itself, she'd run.

CHAPTER 2

The following morning, Cord woke with a start. He'd propped himself up against the wall of the cave near its entrance, one eye on the woman sitting across from him and both ears tuned to any movement outside. She hadn't made a sound all night. He rubbed his eyes. The gray light of dawn filtered through the opening beside him, but shadows still filled the space. He couldn't believe he'd fallen asleep. He hadn't slept during the night since . . .

He shook his head to dispel the demons that haunted him and focused on the problem at hand — the recently deceased Jenny Thompson, owner/editor of *The Angel Ridge Chronicle,* who was very much alive. He'd come up to Laurel Mountain to get in a little hiking before bad weather hit and kept him inside for the rest of the winter. The last thing he'd expected was to find himself on the fringe of a war zone with God only knows who chasing this woman up the side of a mountain intent on killing her.

For a second he wondered what she'd gotten herself tangled up in, but only for a second. He didn't want to know, didn't want to get involved. His focus was on separating himself from this woman, getting supplies and heading back to his cabin before the snow came.

As he stood, the pain in his knees and various other joints reminded him he needed to restock on ibuprofen and muscle rub. He'd run out a few weeks back. He rotated his neck from side to side, the vertebrae popping from top to bottom, releasing some of the tension. His gaze drifted to where the woman sat. She still hadn't moved. He checked his watch. He probably shouldn't risk a fire even though he was desperate for coffee. No way of knowing who might be lurking in the woods, waiting.

Pushing away from the wall of the cave, he said, "Let's get moving."

No response. No movement.

"Hey," he said louder. "Wake up lady. We need to head out."

Cord gathered the few things he had in the cave and began rolling his sleeping bag. The woman was a sound sleeper. He remembered years ago when he'd been able to sleep through anything.

"Hey, sleeping beauty . . . wake up!" He sidestepped to give her a nudge only to realize that his empty coat was the only thing there. He snatched it up like she'd magically appear when he grabbed it. "Crap!"

Outside, he scanned the area. What a crazy, stupid thing for her to do! The woman had a death wish.

He looked in all directions at once, hoping she had just left and he'd see her just outside the cave. No luck. She could have been gone five minutes or five hours. He had no idea how long he'd been asleep. He went back in the cave and finished gathering his things. He slung his pack on one shoulder and went back outside. Fresh tracks led east out of the cave toward the direction she'd come from last night. Could she be crazy enough to go back to that cabin alone?

Heading in the opposite direction and forgetting all about Jenny Thompson held great appeal. He should leave her to whatever trouble she was in, but he found himself jogging down the mountain, retracing his steps to where he'd found her last night. He'd had too many years of training for the instinct to guard and protect to not kick in automatically.

Keeping to the trees, he moved silently because of his familiarity with the terrain. He kept parallel to the trail, hoping that he'd catch up to her. She didn't look like the kind of woman who spent much time hiking the mountains. She'd get lost in the woods, so she'd probably be on the trail, moving along without considering the danger the exposure would pose.

A flash of color teased the edge of his vision and pulled him up short. He edged around a tree, his hand on his gun, and focused on the slash of pale blue against the wide trunk of tree on the other side of the trail. Cord picked up a stick and broke it. The sleeve moved out of sight instantly.

He eased across the trail, then crept up to the tree where she hid, poorly, and snatched out a hand to grab her arm. She sucked in a quick breath, but he covered her mouth before she could scream.

"You're lucky it's me and not someone with a knife intent on slitting your throat," he hissed near her ear.

As soon as he moved his hand away from her mouth, she said, "Did you enjoy that? You nearly gave me a heart attack!"

"What do you think you're doing?"

"Looking for the marshals. They said

43

they'd come find me, so I thought I'd find them instead, somewhere between that cave and the cabin."

"Great idea. Maybe you'll find the guys trying to kill you while you're at it."

"I was being careful."

"I found you in less than five minutes."

"I'm surprised you're awake. I had no trouble getting past you. Both our throats could have been slit while *you* slept."

Towering trees surrounding them filtered the weak morning sunlight, but failed to disguise the features that had been concealed in the darkness last night. She was tall and lean. The sweats she wore only hinted at the curves beneath, but did little to hide long, long legs. Thick blonde hair fell to just below her shoulders, but it was her eyes that drew his attention now. They were a deep dark blue like the water in the Caribbean. A man could get lost in those eyes, if he was so inclined — which he definitely was not.

Jenny wasn't used to looking up to men, even without her heels on, which she was rarely without. But this mystery man was a full half-foot taller than her, making it difficult to read the dark eyes narrowed on her. He'd pulled his long, silky black hair back at the base of his neck, revealing reddish pink scars that starkly contrasted with his dark skin and beard. Everything about him screamed danger. She'd never noticed that about him before, but then he'd never let anyone get near him when he came into Angel Ridge, which wasn't often.

"I've seen you before," she said. "In Angel Ridge. But I don't know your name." And when she'd asked about him, no one would talk. There was nothing she hated more than not knowing. "Who are you?"

"This ain't a social call, lady. I need to get you back to the cave so I can go find your marshals."

She propped a hand on her hip and stood toe to toe with him. "I am quite capable of finding them myself."

"In case you forgot, it's not exactly safe for you out here."

"Or anywhere, it would seem. So what does location matter?"

"Lady, for someone who's supposed to be intelligent, you don't act very smart."

"Jenny."

"I know who you are."

She narrowed her eyes, watching for any signs of subterfuge in his face. "How?"

"I've seen you in town, too. You're kind of hard to miss, especially here. You need a hat. That blonde hair's like a beacon in

45

these gray winter woods."

The first time she'd dyed her hair blonde had been in defiance to her mother who'd thought it improper for a well-raised southern lady. "Trashy" had been the word she'd used to describe it. Dear God . . . the inconsequential things she'd wasted precious time and energy on when she'd had a life and choices.

She gathered her hair, tucked it into her sweatshirt and pulled up the hood. "Better?" she taunted, refusing to acknowledge the critical oversight.

He grunted in lieu of a response. Typical.

"The papers said you were dead."

"You read the paper? That's surprising."

"I'm not about to stand here and waste time swapping insults. Tell me what this is about?"

She folded her arms, but didn't look away. "I can't do that."

"If I'm gonna risk my life to help you, I think I ought to know what I'm getting myself into."

"I didn't ask for your help last night, and I'm not asking for it now."

"That ship's sailed. So just give me the short version."

"I'm not at liberty to give you or anyone else any version."

He looked up giving her a good look at the line of his strong jaw. Her gaze traveled lower to wide shoulders, and she tried not to sigh. He would have to have the two attributes in a man she'd always been unable to resist. Lord, he was beautiful, and the scars only enhanced the beauty by their contrast. Not that it mattered. Nothing mattered anymore.

"Who are you?" she repeated. "If I'm supposed to trust you with my safety, you should at least be willing to tell me your name."

He brought his gaze back to hers. Their eyes locked for a long moment, then finally he said, "Cord."

He grasped her arm and got them moving in what she thought was the direction of the cabin. "Did anyone ever tell you that you're completely lacking in social skills?"

"You're awful free with offering your opinion."

"That wasn't an opinion. That was a fact."

"I don't much care what you think of me, lady. I just want to get you back to those marshals and be on my way."

She jerked her arm out of his grasp. "Again, no one asked for your help."

"Clearly, you're not doing well on your own. You were headed the wrong way, and you're making too much noise. Tread lightly there."

"Stop dragging me along and I will!"

"Women," he grumbled, but released her. "Watch where you're goin'. You're breaking too many sticks. Anybody could hear you from a mile away. Haven't you ever been in the woods?"

As a matter of fact, she hadn't, but she wasn't about to own to it since he clearly considered it a high insult to be lacking in woodsman skills. Still, she couldn't help pricking him a bit. "Unfortunately, that wasn't required for a master's degree in journalism from Vanderbilt."

"Well, if they had taught you something about it, you might not need my help now."

"Are we speaking the same language? No one asked for your help," she said, enunciating each syllable slowly and clearly.

He stopped, pulling her up short. She looked up at him about to tell him to get his hands off her, but he had a finger against his lips then squatted, pulling her down next to him. He pointed at something ahead.

Jenny could still smell the acrid scent of gunfire in the heavy, humid morning air, bringing all she'd experienced last night back in a rush.

"Stay here."

Keeping low, he skirted the clearing where the cabin stood, keeping in the cover of the trees surrounding it. He scanned the area for any movement that might signal that someone was still nearby. Watching, waiting . . .

The small cabin was riddled with bullet holes. The door stood open. He scanned the area again, then pulling a gun from the waistband of his pants, crouched low and got quickly inside. He immediately went to a man lying prone on the floor just inside.

"Is he . . ."

Cord swung around, pointing the gun at her. Jenny held up her hands. "Easy." She slowly moved into the room, keeping against the wall.

"I told you to stay put."

"I had to see for myself if they . . . if they were okay."

Cord stood. "There's no helping him."

He looked at her then. His expression was cold as stone. Jenny shivered and pressed the back of her hand to her mouth.

"If you're gonna be sick —"

"I'm fine," she insisted, though she looked anything but.

"How many marshals were here with you?"

"Two when I left."

"Did they radio for help?"

"I don't know. It all happened so fast. They got me into a tunnel leading away from here as soon as the gunfire started."

He moved into the back room, and Jenny followed. They found Pierce in the middle of the room. Blood stained the floor and walls. He lay on his back, gray and lifeless . . . a chest wound darkened his t-shirt. Jenny backed away from the dead man until the wall stopped her progress. She rubbed her arms, looking around the room, anywhere but at the man who'd helped her into the tunnel last night. When she felt a hand on her shoulder, she jumped, surprised to see Cord towering over her.

He shook her a little. "The last thing I need right now is for you to go into shock."

"They're dead because of me, so forgive me if I go all girly and get emotional."

"Whatever went down here, that's over."

How could he be so cold and unfeeling? She looked back at Pierce, and bile rushed into the back of her throat. She turned and threw up in the corner of the room. When she'd emptied the meager contents of her stomach, she straightened, her hand covering her mouth. Cord was right. She did need to get out of here.

"Did the marshals have a radio?"

She nodded, but couldn't speak through her constricted throat.

Cord looked around the room, moved a few things, rolled the dead man over, like he was inconsequential, looking for the radio. When his search brought up nothing, he went into the other room.

Gunfire vibrated the walls of the cabin. Jenny crouched in the corner of the room, her eyes squeezed shut. Cord rushed back from the other room, and shut the door, sliding the bar lock home. "I need you out of here. You said something about a tunnel?"

Jenny nodded, still unable to speak.

"Where?"

She pointed at Pierce. He got the message. Ducking to avoid the window, he moved over to the marshal and pulled him back out of the way. He moved a blood-soaked rug, exposing a door in the floor. He opened it then looked back at her. He motioned her over with his gun. No. Not again . . .

He pulled a flashlight from his pack and tossed it to her. "Go back to the cave where we stayed last night and wait for me."

Her gaze moved from the dead marshal and back to him. "No."

"Don't argue. Move."

51

She got moving, but instead of doing as he said, she grabbed his hand to get his full attention. "What if you die, too?"

His gaze intense, he squeezed her hand. "I'll come for you."

She tilted her head toward the dead man in the room. "He said the same thing."

Someone rattled the doorknob, and Jenny wrapped her arm around his. He instinctively turned to put her behind him, then they started pounding something against the door. It gave with every blow.

"Go."

He helped her into the tunnel. The door above her closed. She crouched there several moments listening, but heard nothing other than the pounding on the door. She pushed the hood back off her head, raking a hand through her hair. Would this nightmare never end? The door to the room crashed open, and like last night, Jenny began to move.

CHAPTER 3

Jenny quickly made her way through the tunnel. It didn't take nearly as long as it had seemed last night. The door at the end opened more easily this time. She closed and concealed it as she had before.

She darted behind some trees and looked back at the cabin in the clearing below. The first thing that registered was the quiet. No gunfire. Jenny watched as a dirty group of men in camouflage gathered outside the cabin. One man's voice carried above the rest.

"They just disappeared. We saw them go in, but no one came out."

"Don't give me that bull crap about haints and such. You think the boss is gonna buy that when two of his men is dead in there?"

The largest man shoved one of the other men to the ground, then turned. He scanned the area around him. His gaze stopped. He looked right at her. Jenny slowly sank behind a tree, concealing herself completely. Her hair; she'd forgotten. Again! Pulling the hood up, she closed her eyes.

Someone grabbed her from behind. A strong arm banded her waist and a large, gloved hand covered her mouth. The man pressed his lips to her ear. Fear and awareness coursed through her body.

"I told you to go to the cave."

Weak with relief, she pried Cord's hand off her mouth. "I just got out of the tunnel."

"There! I saw something move up there," one of the men at the cabin shouted.

They didn't move. Jenny didn't breathe, but she was aware of the danger and every hard, square inch of the man whose body was pressed up against her from shoulder to ankle.

"Probably just a squirrel."

"Check it out!"

"Aw, hell," Cord said, then grabbed her hand and ran.

"There she is!"

"There's someone with her."

They darted into the trees. Cord shoved her into the crevice of a rock, then pulled a knife with a long, thick silver blade from its holder on his belt, cut some branches from a bush and covered her up. When concealed, all she could see was the feral look in his dark eyes as he placed the last branch in front of her.

Her breathing sounded unnaturally loud in the silence. Then they came, thrashing up the trail.

"Their tracks end here."

"Spread out."

Jenny put her hands over her nose and mouth and made herself as small as possible. She saw a man with an assault rifle approach. He poked every bush with his weapon. He was headed right for her. Cord silently came between the man and her. Then almost immediately, the man went limp. Cord threw him over his shoulder, and blended silently into the landscape.

Two more men appeared. "Where's Bob?"

"I don't know. Probably back at the cabin. There's no one here."

"Yeah, you're right. This is a waste of time."

"She's gotta come off this mountain sometime."

"And we'll be there when she does."

"Yeah, puttin' a bullet in her's gonna be a real pleasure."

Crude laughter trailed behind them as they retraced their steps to the cabin. Watching the men walk away, she should have felt relief, but instead terror clinched her chest. Closing her eyes, she couldn't stop the replay of Cord so easily taking that man out, like he'd done it before.

That knowledge brought home the fact that she knew nothing about this man. She'd spent the night with him. Had even been irrationally attracted to him. She rubbed her forehead, trying to think clearly. He hadn't tried to harm her. She'd never find her way off this mountain without him. He was her only hope for getting out alive. Still, one fact outweighed all the rest . . .

He might have just killed a man.

Jenny didn't know how long she sat there, shivering against the rock in the freezing cold. She looked around the clearing. Where was he? Would he come back for her? Did she want him to? Her mind churned with the reality of the danger she faced from the men pursuing her and the dangerous man she had to trust to help her get back to civilization. And then there were the marshals who, up to now, had failed miserably at keeping her safe. She couldn't help thinking how much better off she'd be on her own.

Someone began dismantling the brush covering her. Before Jenny could react, her arm felt like it had been placed in a vice grip. "Let's get moving."

Her heart barely had time to begin beating again before she was pulled upright to stand in front of the man she both feared and needed. "Lord, would you stop doing that? I had no idea who had just found me!"

"We don't have time for this."

She looked down at his hand, remembering what he'd done.

"Did you kill that man?" The question was out before she could stop it.

"Let's go," he said, pulling her along behind him.

"You didn't answer my question."

"You talk more than anybody I ever knew. He's fine. He'll wake up in an hour or so with the worst headache of his life. He deserves a lot worse."

He moved them into a dense copse of trees. There was no path, but like before, Cord weaved through them like he knew the way. "How do I know you're telling the truth? You could have killed him. You had a knife."

Stopping, he brought her up short and pinned her with an icy glare. "You watch too much TV. First, I'm not a cop. I can't just kill a man because 'I can' without there being consequences, and I don't plan to go to jail. Second, there was no reason to kill him. I just needed him out of the way."

"Where did you learn how to do that?"

Cord sighed. "I can take care of myself. Look, if you're finished with your interrogation, we need to get out of here."

She nodded. "Of course."

He began walking again, and she followed. "Where are we going?" she asked.

His sigh was loud enough to echo through the trees. "I have a car. If we make good time, we should reach it by noon."

She'd run there if it meant she could be away from this present danger and safe again. "Safe" being a relative term. She hadn't been safe since she'd stumbled on this crime ring.

What the hell were the police and federal agents who were supposed to be making arrests doing? Grady said he'd see that enough people were put away that she might even be able to come home, but every time she turned around, it seemed a dozen or more men were gunning for her. That had to mean it was more involved than they'd first thought. She'd done her best to get up to date information from the marshals by eavesdropping on their conversations, but had learned nothing.

For now, she'd follow this man off the

mountain and into what was sure to be another precarious situation. Once he got her back to civilization, she'd make a run for it. How could she be worse off on her own?

They'd been walking for several hours in blessed silence, giving Cord a chance to reassess their situation. He'd clearly misjudged things. He didn't have many facts, but he didn't like what he knew. Jenny had to be in some phase of witness protection if she was in the custody of U.S. Marshals. Fine. His plan had been to turn her back over to them. But with them dead and their killers still on this mountain and looking for her, that wasn't happening here.

How could a woman like her be in so much trouble? He'd read *The Chronicle.* It wasn't known for hard-hitting investigative pieces. Just a bunch of small town, local interest pieces mostly. Besides that, there was no crime in Angel Ridge other than a few recent break-ins and the explosion that had leveled the newspaper.

No matter. He'd get back to his car and call Angel Ridge's sheriff. With any luck, he'd drop her off, pick up his supplies in town and get to his cabin by nightfall. He didn't plan on venturing out again until spring.

He was just about to turn and check on how Jenny was doing when a bullet whizzed past him and lodged in a tree. He instinctively moved to protect her, but she was prone with her hands over her head. "Get up."

Before she had time to react, he got his gun out of his waistband, hauled her to her feet, and pulled her along behind him as he sprinted over to an outcropping of rocks. He crouched behind one and got her down to her knees. A man with a rifle appeared where they had just been standing and looked around.

"Hey, Luke. That you?"

He was wearing a bright orange hunter's jacket and a camouflage hat with ear flaps.

Another man appeared. "Back here, man."

"Damn. My rifle misfired. Glad you was behind me."

The hunter named Luke laughed drunkenly and slapped his buddy on the back. "Let's find a couple of trees for our deer stands."

They shuffled off in the opposite direction, and Jenny slumped against him. After a moment he said, "Just a couple of drunken hunters."

Jenny nodded. "Yeah. Harmless in comparison to those other guys, huh?"

"Well, I don't know if I'd call two drunks with guns harmless."

She looked up at him, smiling. "That was sarcasm."

Ignoring that, he made sure no one else was coming. Jenny seemed tired, but they weren't far from the parking area at the trailhead. She could rest in his car. Regardless, he found himself asking, "You all right to keep going?"

"Of course."

He made the mistake of looking back at her. Her eyes were bright with unshed tears. Great. Whether her reaction was from fear, frustration, or exhaustion, he didn't know. He offered a hand, and she surprised him by taking it despite her obvious mistrust of him, which he had to admit he admired. She *should* mistrust a total stranger.

He helped her up, and she followed him over to a stream he knew was nearby. She sat on a rock as he fished a bottle of water out of his pack. "Here."

"Thanks." She took it and drank half in one pull. "How much further?"

"Not far. Ten, maybe fifteen minutes."

"What happens when we get to your car?"

"We'll be back in cell range, so I'll call the

sheriff over in Angel Ridge."

She nodded and drank the rest of the water. "Let's go then."

She stood and walked over to him. Cord watched. She was a fine-looking woman . . . "It can wait." He looked out across the stream and up at the sky, heavy with snow-filled clouds. "It's kinda peaceful here."

She looked up at the sky, too. After a few moments had passed, she whispered, "That can change quickly. We just saw that."

"For what it's worth, they never should have had you on this mountain. It's too close to Angel Ridge."

"Is it? I didn't know. Doesn't surprise me, though. They tried everything. Guess they thought no one would look for me so close to Angel Ridge."

The sound of the stream flowing by soothed, but looking at Jenny, he saw that nothing could put her at ease right now. Maybe they'd make enough arrests that she'd get her old life back. It might happen, but he knew it wasn't likely.

They stood there for several moments allowing the sound of the stream to wash over them. Finally, Cord said, "We can go whenever you're ready."

She nodded and smoothed her hands over

her hips, then rubbed her arms. "It's getting colder."

He shrugged out of his coat and handed it to her. She held up a hand.

She shook her head. "I'm fine."

"It's okay. I have a pullover in my pack."

After a moment, she accepted it and said, "Thank you."

Cord had to look away from her smile. It warmed him like the summer sun. He couldn't go there. Wouldn't go there.

Without speaking or looking at her, he hefted his pack and walked back into the woods. The sound of footsteps behind him and her scent his only assurance that she followed. The sooner he turned her over, the better. Prolonged involvement with Jenny Thompson would complicate his life. He didn't need more complications.

CHAPTER 4

"I'd be happy to speak with you, but now's just not a good time."

"I haven't had an update on my sister since they took her into protective custody, Sheriff. Surely you can spare five minutes."

The pleading, soft look in the pretty brunette's blue eyes spoke to him. Other than the hair color, she looked just like Jenny.

"Ms. Thompson, I will answer any questions you have. It's just that we've had an emergency that requires my immediate attention. I'm sure you understand. My assistant, Clara," he stood and raised his voice a bit when he said his clerk's name, and like an angel, she appeared in his office door. "Ah, here she is. Clara, this is Jenny Thompson's sister, Frances."

"Frannie, please."

Grady gritted his teeth, more than smiled. He didn't have time for pleasantries and politeness. So he just nodded and moved towards the door, hoping she would follow.

She did, but said softly enough so that only he could hear, "Sheriff, I know two months have passed and it's likely that you and everyone else in this town has forgotten all about my sister, but as you know, she and her family have made quite a sacrifice so this town and the people in it can be safe."

Grady's sigh was heartfelt. He'd woken up this morning with a funny feeling in his gut. Lark, or Candi as everyone else called her, had told him that the snowstorm due to hit today would be the worst for East Tennessee in more than a decade. Beyond that, he'd had a feeling that all hell was about to break loose in the case he'd been working with other state and federal agencies since Jenny had been taken into protective custody.

And sure enough, his cell phone and scanner had lit up like a Christmas tree about three this morning. The incompetence of U.S. Marshal Service knew no bounds. In all their wisdom, they had decided to hide Jenny in a hikers' cabin on Laurel Mountain, of all places, on just the other side of the lake from Angel Ridge, never mind that Jenny had had to sign an agreement that she would never come back here. Apparently, that did not preclude them from keeping her within spitting distance of the town she'd been taken from.

Now, these hills were crawling with remnants of the crime syndicate Jenny had uncovered after Lark came to town this past fall to open up her business. These backwoods thugs had been re-enlisted to help flush Jenny out. The cabin Jenny had been held in last night had gotten shot up. Two marshals and two unidentified men were dead in his jurisdiction. To top it off, Jenny was missing. Even now, the highway patrol had a roadblock set up trying to find her. Like the people looking for her weren't following local law enforcement's every move.

In short, he had more trouble than a dog had fleas, and on top of it, Jenny's sister was here in town at the worst possible time. She could never know that Jenny had been found everywhere the marshals had hidden her, and that it was a miracle she was still alive. Miss Estelee would say "when it rains it pours," but Frannie was a complication he didn't need right now.

"Grady, did you know there's a roadblock — oh, I'm sorry," Fuzz Rhoton said. "I didn't know you were busy."

Fuzz pulled up short in the doorway to

his office just behind Clara. "Ms. Thompson," he said, "this is Fuzz Rhoton. He helps out from time to time when the sheriff's office needs extra hands."

"And are you in need of extra hands now, Sheriff?" Frannie asked.

"As I said, there is a situation that needs my attention." To Fuzz he said, "Could you go pick up the constable? With this storm, I have a feeling we're going to need all hands on deck today and tonight." He gave the man a meaningful look, hoping he got the underlying message.

Fuzz nodded, eyebrows raised, indicating he understood. "Of course. I'll do that now."

The man turned and headed back outside. "Clara, would you mind showing Ms. Thompson to the diner? Y'all could have a cup of coffee and a piece of pie while I take care of my pressing business. I'll get there as soon as I can to continue our conversation." He put his hat on. To his deputy, he said, "Woody, you stay here and hold down the fort. I'll check in."

"Sure thing, Boss," the deputy agreed.

Grady edged around everyone and out the door. His cell phone rang before he made it to his Jeep. "Wallace."

"Sheriff, this is Cordell Goins."

Grady pulled the phone back from his ear

and checked the caller ID. The display read, "C. Goins." This day was just full of surprises. Why in the world would Goins be calling him? He'd been in the area for years and had never spoken to him until now.

"Goins. This is a surprise. Everything all right out your way?"

"I wouldn't know. I've been hikin' for the better part of a week."

"Good time for it. You're likely to be confined to that mountain you live on for a good while after the snow comes, not that I can imagine that bothers you near as much as it does most."

"Sheriff, if you don't mind, I have a matter of importance to discuss."

All right then. "I apologize. State your business."

"I was hiking up on Laurel Mountain last night and ran into some trouble."

Great. "I can imagine you did. There's a unit of state and federal officers headed that way."

"They'd be about a day too late."

"No survivors then?" He didn't want to say too much. Still, he prayed Jenny was all right.

"Only one that matters."

"Male or female?"

"Female."

68

Grady let out the breath he'd been holding.

"I was thinking to pay you a call."

"Negative." If Goins had Jenny, he could not bring her to town. Even if he got through the roadblock, they couldn't risk Jenny being seen by her sister. "I'll come to you. What's your location?"

"Trailhead parking lot for Laurel Mountain, but it's no good meeting here, if you get my meanin'."

"I do."

"Sheriff, I need to pick up supplies before this bad weather lays in. If I could kill two birds —"

"You and everyone else in East Tennessee. Meet me at the Wal-Mart just outside of town."

"All right. I'll park outside the garden center. I'm in an older dark Jeep Wrangler."

"I'll find you. And Goins?"

"Yeah."

"You're likely to hit a roadblock before you get to that shopping center. Think you can handle that?"

Goins let loose several curses before replying that he could. "Be there soon as I can."

Grady put his hat on the seat next to him and drove as fast as he dared out of Angel Ridge. He didn't need to draw attention and have anyone follow.

The sky was overcast and heavy with moisture. The temperature had dropped even more. Jenny pulled Cord's coat closer around her. She pressed her back to the tree where he'd left her while he scouted the parking area at the trailhead. If she knew how to hotwire a car, she'd be out of here. Lord how she hated being at the mercy of others — particularly men. She was an independent, competent woman accustomed to taking care of herself. But since the explosion, she'd been at the mercy of a string of people who could barely read a map much less keep her safe, not that a lot of the area around Angel Ridge was even on a map.

And now she was with this man, Cord . . . On the one hand she wasn't sure she should trust him and frankly, he terrified her. On the other hand, he'd helped her, if grudgingly. He was the most compelling and mysterious man she'd ever encountered. Even with the few times she'd seen him in town, she'd been curious about him, but he kept to himself and talked to no one. When she'd asked Dixie about him — and Dixie knew everything about everyone in and around Angel Ridge — she'd gotten next to nothing. Just that he lived in the mountains and kept to himself.

The man had secrets, no doubt, and there was nothing that intrigued her more than a mystery that begged solving, but she no longer had that luxury. If she would survive this, she couldn't get distracted by an uncommunicative mystery man. She had to stay focused. Only a couple of facts about Cord mattered. One, he knew how to kill a man, and two, she couldn't give her trust to a man she knew nothing about. Furthermore, the marshals had proven over and over that they couldn't keep her safe. So, she was going to have to find a way to take matters into her own hands.

"Jenny?"

She nearly jumped out of her skin when Cord touched her shoulder.

Good Lord, the man moved like a cat. With a tree between them, the result was a nasty scrape across her cheek as she jerked away from him. She touched a hand to her stinging face and looked at it. Blood smeared her fingertips. "Dang it!"

"Sorry."

Before she could move away, he'd reached into his pocket, removed a bandana, and pressed it to her cheek. Jenny took the handkerchief and moved away from his touch. She needed to keep a clear head.

"Is it safe? Can we go?" she asked, looking around as she had been the entire time he'd been gone.

"That needs cleanin'."

"I'm fine."

"What's this?"

"What?"

"These." He lifted her hands, displaying the scrapes crisscrossing her palms, the result of her struggling through the earthen tunnel twice. "Looks like you have splinters that have already started to fester. I have a first aid kit in my pack."

Jenny shoved her hands in her coat pockets. "I can do it while you drive." Turning the conversation back to the task at hand, she asked, "What's the plan?"

He nodded and looked away. Had she seen a flash of emotion in his cold dark eyes? What was that about?

"I'm taking you to meet the sheriff at a shopping center outside Angel Ridge."

"Grady Wallace?"

"Yeah. I called him when I got to the car. You'll have to hide in the back of my Jeep because there could be a roadblock between here and there."

"That doesn't sound at all safe."

He stared up at the sky, still not looking

at her. "It isn't."

Jenny laughed harshly. "Of course it's not. It's not safe for me anywhere around here."

"The sheriff will correct that as soon as I get you to him. We should go. The longer we wait, the more likely we are to encounter other hikers."

"Or the people looking for me. They probably have the parking lot staked out."

"Could be, but you can't stay here."

Jenny pressed the fear down. "Let's go, then."

He reached behind her and pulled up the hood of the coat so that it covered her hair and partially concealed her face. "Keep your head down."

Cord pulled a ball cap low over his eyes. He turned to lead the way down to the parking area, then decided to make it look like they were a couple to throw off anyone who might be watching. He took Jenny's hand, lacing his fingers with hers. She looked at him, surprised. "Just play along," he said softly.

She cooperated and didn't try to pull away. They quickly emerged from the woods at his Jeep. He unlocked her door and helped her in, then came around and got in on his side. The gloom of the coming snow hung over them like an ominous warning.

He tossed her the first aid kit before putting his pack in the back, and then said, "Crawl back behind my seat. It's pretty junky, but you can clear out a spot and pile some blankets on top of you."

Jenny hesitated. She looked over her shoulder at the tangle of blankets, fishing tackle, hunting fatigues, and a gas can. She tried not to wrinkle her nose and wondered for the thousandth time in the past couple of months how this had become her life.

"Is there a problem?"

"No."

"Then get into the back before someone sees you."

He checked the mirrors and the parking lot. Back to reality . . . and her companion's surliness. Despite the camaraderie she'd felt developing between them at the creek and the easy way they'd held hands, as soon as they'd gotten in the car, he'd gone all intense, clearly intent on unloading her so he could be on his way.

Jenny did as he said. As she moved things around trying to get settled, her mind did what it had always done; churned with questions.

"Can I ask you something?"

No response, but she forged ahead, like she always did. She'd made a career out of coaxing answers from reluctant people. Cord was just another person for her to work her magic on. "How'd you get out of the cabin? Did you use the tunnel?"

"No."

"Then how?"

He paused a long moment, then said, "What difference does it make? Are you set back there?"

It made all the difference. She had to have answers. They were all she had now. "Almost, and humor me," she said with a smile. Even though he couldn't see it, maybe he could hear it and would feel comfortable enough to answer.

Silence. Then Cord muttered a blistering expletive and started the car.

"What is it?"

"Stay down and be quiet."

He put the car in gear and got them moving. Jenny tried to find something to hold onto as he took a curve out of the parking lot onto the road and hit the gas. She slid across the back of the Jeep into something solid and grunted as a sharp pain pierced her side. Jenny wedged her feet against one panel of the car with her shoulders pressed up against the other panel. She held her side as pain tore through her midsection.

"You all right?" he muttered.

"No," she said through clinched teeth. "Not that it matters."

"Sorry," he grumbled.

"What happened?"

"It didn't feel right."

"Did you see someone?"

No response.

Still holding her side, she eased up so she could look out the window. Maybe someone was following them.

"Are you crazy? Get down! The roadblock is just ahead. Cover up and don't move."

"What if they decide to search the car?"

"They won't."

"If they're looking for me, they likely will."

"Settle down and be quiet."

Cord got in the line of stopped cars and waited as the patrolmen spoke to each driver and then let them go. Car after car moved up and pulled out. Finally, he pulled up alongside the highway patrolman standing in the road. Since he didn't have a traditional window in the Jeep, he opened his door and stepped out. "Morning, officer. Mighty cold morning for a roadblock," he said, hunching his shoulders against the wind while he scanned the tree-lined roadside.

"Mornin'. We'd like to see your license and registration." The officer looked over the car. "This sure is some vehicle."

"Thanks," Cord said as he handed over the requested documents.

" '65?"

" '66."

"Wrangler CJ-5?"

"Yeah."

"You've took real good care of it."

"Yes, sir."

"Everything seems to be in order here. Where you headed?"

"Home."

"Looks like you been hiking," the officer said, looking at the backpack behind the passenger seat. Cord shifted to block the man's view of anything further.

"Yes, sir."

"Where 'bouts?

"Up around Elkmont," Cord lied.

"We been looking for a little lady that got lost up on Laurel Mountain. Haven't seen any strangers on the road have you?"

"Hard to say with as many tourists as we get around here this time of year." Cord forced himself to be calm when the deputy shined a flashlight inside the Jeep.

"Bein's you've been out of touch while you were hiking, I guess you ain't heard about the storm headed this way."

Any idiot with eyes in their head could

tell there was a storm coming, but he said, "No, sir."

"Yep." The big man hooked his thumbs in his gun belt and rocked back on his heels. "Big snowstorm. They're predictin' it might rival the '93 blizzard. But you know, when they're callin' for it, we usually don't get a drop. Just the same, it might be smart if you stock up before you head home. Up where you live, you won't be getting out for awhile if there's bad weather."

That was the plan, just as soon as he dropped off his unwanted guest. "Thanks. I'll do that."

"All righty. If you see any strangers around, anybody suspicious lookin', we'd appreciate you givin' us a call."

"Will do." Cord got back into the Jeep and wasted no time putting the car in gear.

When they were on their way, Jenny peeped out from under the blankets and sneezed about a half dozen times. "I didn't think I was going to make it. These things you call blankets are stiff with dust!"

"Keep your head down," Cord mumbled.

"Stop barking orders at me. I'm no happier to be with you than you are having me."

Ignoring that, Cord retreated into his thoughts. How stupid could you get? If this was how the police were handling such a sensitive situation, what would happen to her when he turned her over to the sheriff's department? He looked out the windshield up at the sky. The first snowflakes floated down. If he left her in Angel Ridge, she'd get snowed in there. With blood-thirsty criminals crawling all over the area, she'd be a sitting duck.

Jenny sniffed. "What are you thinking?"

"Anybody ever tell you that you ask too many questions?" He could barely hear himself think, she talked so much.

"Occupational hazard."

What did he care if she lived or died? It was none of his concern after he turned her over to the sheriff. He'd go back to his cabin and forget all about her. He looked over his shoulder and their gazes met. Her unguarded blue eyes looked huge in her pale face. Dark smudges under her eyes told of too many sleepless nights. His heart constricted involuntarily. How could anyone want to harm anything so gut-clinching gorgeous?

He dragged a hand down his face. How had that happened? He wanted her to be safe, and he hadn't cared about anything or anyone in a long time.

"There's a snowstorm coming."

"We've established that."

"I don't know who these people are that want to harm you, but they're determined to get to you. Being snowed in so close to where we last saw them is suicide."

"That's not your concern. All you have to do is turn me over to Grady and be on your way."

"When it snows, I can't get off the mountain where I live, sometimes for weeks. If a blizzard hits, who knows?"

Cord looked in his mirror and saw Jenny roll onto her back. The movement stirred up more dust.

Somewhere between sneezes, she managed to say, "Sounds perfect . . . for you."

"If I can't get out, no one can get in." He reached into the glove box, grabbed some napkins, and handed them to her. Jenny blew — an inelegant sound. Cord couldn't help smiling.

"If there's a point to this, state it."

"You could hide out at my place. No one would ever find you there. If these people lose your trail, maybe they'll give up and go back to where they came from."

Jenny laughed.

"What's so funny?"

"That's the worst idea I've ever heard."

"I'm sure the sheriff will agree."

"I'm sure he won't, not if I have anything

to say about it. Let me tell you one thing —
there is no way in hell I'm holing up in some
cabin in the middle of nowhere, snowed in
for God knows how long, with you."

"Why not?"

"It's not happening. I can't believe you'd
suggest such a thing."

"It's the safest option for you. If the sheriff
takes you back to Angel Ridge, you're sure
to get stuck there, and that's the worst possible scenario right now."

Jenny sat up. "Are you saying you're not
taking me to Grady?"

No response.

"What if it doesn't snow?"

"It's already started."

"It could blow over or turn out to be just
this. A few flurries."

"I've lived in the mountains most of my
life. I know the signs. It's not blowing over."

"No. Take me to the sheriff like we
planned."

"You'd be safe at my cabin."

She folded her arms across her chest.
"No."

"It's remote. There's no one and nothing
for miles, no phone, no mail."

"No electricity."

"I have electricity."

"We'd kill each other inside of twenty

minutes."

He waited before he spoke, weighing his words carefully. "If it means you live to see another spring, I'm willing to tolerate you if you're willing to tolerate me."

"What do you care if I live or die? Turn me over to Grady and be on your way."

"I can't do that." Hearing the words, it sounded like someone else talking.

"Why not?"

He could tell from the edge in her tone that she was frustrated and focused on getting away from him. From everyone. He'd heard it before when he was in the military and then later in the bureau, transporting prisoners, officers and civilians. When things went bad, this happened. Jenny was there. Desperation. That made her a danger to herself and everyone around her. What if she ran when the sheriff got her to Angel Ridge? What if she wound up dead?

He sighed and said, "I have to live with myself. That's why." It was one thing to have to live with an op that had gone bad. He had the nightmares to prove it. It was another thing when he knew what to do to save someone and willingly walked away. That was not an option.

He glanced over his shoulder and caught her nervously chewing on her thumbnail.

"You know I'm right," he pressed

She glanced up at him, then focused on the side of the Jeep again. "I want to talk to Grady."

"You'll get your chance soon enough."

"I am not, do you hear me, *not* going to hole up in a remote cabin with you for the foreseeable future."

"It's either me or the next set of marshals. Your luck with them, up to now, hasn't been so good."

"Right, so why would my luck be any better with you? No. I won't do it."

He gripped the wheel and said between his teeth, "Has anyone ever told you that you are a frustratingly difficult woman?"

"Yeah. It's just one of the many things that makes me good at what I do."

"Correct me if I'm wrong, but the only thing you have to do now is try to stay alive."

The only sound for several minutes was the engine, the tires turning on the pavement and his own breathing. "Jenny, think about what I'm suggesting. You could be safe for the first time in weeks."

"What if they need me to appear at trial and I can't get out to testify? And if they did find us, what would we do? No one could get there quickly enough to help us."

He almost laughed. He couldn't remember the last time he'd had the urge to laugh. "Do you ever ask just one question at a time?"

"Only if I like you," she fired back.

Cord was glad she couldn't see him smile. He was sure it was so rusty it creaked audibly. "They won't find us, and I can get out if I want to. It's just that usually, I don't want to."

"That's why this makes no sense. Why do you care what happens to me?"

He thought for a minute before he said, "It's the right thing to do."

"Lord, do they breed that in to southern men or what?"

It sounded like she was talking to herself.

"Look, I know this is hard —"

"You have no idea. Try not having control of your own destiny for even five minutes."

"You've put your trust in a lot of people who didn't deserve it, but I'll see that you're taken care of now."

She laughed. She was actually laughing? "What's so funny?"

"I can't remember a day in my life that I needed 'taking care of'. I'm the one that takes care of everyone, including myself." She paused, then added, "This is absurd. How can this be my life? I've been reduced to someone with absolutely no control over her own fate and as a bonus, I can't trust anyone either."

Her words had gone all soft so that he could hardly make out the last words over the hum of the engine. He looked in the rearview. She had her hands on both sides of her head and her eyes were closed.

"You can trust me," he whispered. No matter how that promise might be tested, he knew he'd do whatever it took to keep her safe. This time would be different.

CHAPTER 5

"Come in folks, come in," Dixie invited.

Snow blew Clara and a familiar-looking stranger into the deserted diner.

"This snowstorm's coming on stronger than a buck in a herd of does in heat! Have a seat here at the counter."

"Dixie, this is Jenny Thompson's sister, Frances," Clara said.

The young brunette who looked so much like her sister came forward, hand extended. "Frannie, please. You must be Dixie. My sister spoke fondly of you."

Dixie so hated promoting this lie, but knew that it was best for everyone concerned. "Frannie." She took the young woman's hand in both of hers. "Of course, we met briefly at the memorial service, but I'm sure you met so many people that day . . ."

"I do remember the food you provided looked wonderful."

Dixie nodded. "Jenny spoke of you so often, I feel like I already know you. I'm so sorry for your loss," she added, and she was truly sorry. Regardless of whether or not Jenny was actually dead, she was gone forever to her sister and everyone who loved her.

"Thank you."

"Let me get you some coffee," Dixie suggested, setting thick white mugs in front of the two women. "With this snowstorm rolling in so fast, I was just bagging up the special thinking that folks might want to take something with them on their way home. As you can see, my lunch crowd has fled. I've got stew and cornbread muffins."

"Sounds good," Frannie said.

"How about you, Clara?"

"Your stew always hits the spot. Thanks, Dixie."

"You're a dear, Clara. Coming right up."

Dixie poured the coffee, then turned to dish up two bowls of soup from a crock pot. She placed cornbread muffins on a plate and put it all on the counter in front of Frannie and Clara.

"I hope you don't mind, but the sheriff asked me to wait here for him. He had some business to take care of before he could speak with me about my sister's . . . *um,* her —"

"Accident," Dixie supplied.

"Is that what folks around here are calling it?" Frannie asked.

"Well, folks around here haven't said much at all since the memorial service, like we're all supposed to go on like nothing happened."

Fuzz Rhoton sidled up to the bar and leaned in. "If you ask me, I don't think it was an accident at all."

Dixie cocked a hand on her hip. "Well, hello Fuzz. I didn't see you come in."

Fuzz thumbed in the direction of Henry Harris who was just joining them at the lunch counter. "Sheriff asked me to find the Constable, and I figured he'd be here having lunch."

"Wouldn't miss it," Henry chimed in.

"Not since I took over the diner from my folks has he missed a meal, not unless he's in bed sick, and then he calls for delivery."

Henry chuckled, but Fuzz steered the conversation back by saying, "I didn't mean to interrupt, but if you don't mind me sayin', none of the facts of what happened to your sister adds up."

Frannie said nothing, so deciding to play along so as not to arouse suspicion, Dixie said, "I'm sure it's nothing folks haven't been thinking for months."

"I don't think it's a good idea to speculate," Clara interjected, looking very uncomfortable with the direction the conversation had taken.

Dixie laughed. "Since when did you know me to not speculate? I mean, this whole thing shouts conspiracy theory, and you know I love a good conspiracy theory."

"Hold on there, Dixie. Did I hear you right? Did you say 'conspiracy theory'?"

"Fuzz, it's like you said, and you know as well as anybody things don't add up in all of this since you were helping out the sheriff's department when all of that mess of break-ins and reckless driving incidents were going on last fall. Who ever heard of a gas line explosion that only takes out one office in a line of buildings that are all connected?"

Frannie sat listening carefully, eyes wide.

"I'd say I'm not qualified to make such an assessment," Fuzz said, "but I can tell you that a number of agencies from local law enforcement assessed the damage at the newspaper, and we have to believe that what they said was accurate."

"*Mm-hmm.* What I'm saying is that I have a brain in my head, and I'm capable of drawing my own conclusions. It makes no sense. Just like we know that Marilyn Monroe didn't kill herself. You know that Frank Sinatra had her killed because she knew too much about his connections to the mob. And you further know that Prince Phillip had Princess Diana killed because, Lord knows, you can't have the future king of England being raised by a Muslim. Drunk driver, my hind leg. Plus they hated Princess Di. She was gorgeous and they all look like horses. And for the love of Kenny Chesney, if you are the Queen of England, can you not buy a cute purse? She has been carrying the same hideous bag for the past forty years —"

Fuzz held up his hand, halting the steady stream of words. "Could we bring this back to the explosion at the newspaper?"

"Oh, sorry. I do get carried away."

"You know, it was right after Candi Heart moved to town that a string of crimes was committed. I never seen anything like it around here."

"Really?" Frannie said.

Since he brought it up, Dixie nodded, leaning a hip against the counter. "Candi came to town and within a month, there was a reckless driving incident where Candi and the sheriff were nearly killed, and

Candi's shop was broken into twice before she even had her grand opening."

"And I heard that some hateful things were spray painted on the walls of her shop," Fuzz added.

"Were these crimes investigated?" Frannie asked.

"Of course," Clara said.

"And were any arrests made?"

"That's the thing," Fuzz said, "no arrests were ever made."

"The investigation is ongoing," Clara corrected.

"That's why I'm here," Frannie said. "To find out what has happened since — since the explosion."

"If you ask me, I believe there's a connection to all that happened with Candi Heart last fall and the explosion that killed Jenny Thompson," Fuzz said.

"No one asked you, Fuzz," Clara said, giving the man a pointed look.

"Have there been any more incidents of crime in town since the explosion?"

"No," Dixie replied. "Like I said, things have been real quiet around here."

"Strange if you ask me. Seems like they got the one they wanted to keep quiet and left," Fuzz said.

"Again, no one asked you, Fuzz," Clara

pointed out.

"Anyway, we all miss Jenny very much, and we are so, so sorry for your loss. I hope we haven't upset you with our crazy talk. The bottom line is that your sister was an amazing woman. She made a positive impact on this town, and she was a role model for the young girls around here." She took Frannie's hand. "I miss her more than I can say."

A mist of tears filled Dixie's eyes. She pulled a napkin out of one of the holders on the counter and dabbed at the moistness. Frannie leaned over and squeezed her arm. The two women looked at each other, Frannie's eyes so much like her sister's, and an instant bond formed between the two.

"Anyway, if I can be of any help to you while you're in town, please don't hesitate to come to me. Given the fact that I run the only diner in town, pretty much all of Angel Ridge comes through here. I know something about just about everyone and everything."

"That's the truth," Fuzz commented.

"Fuzz, in this kind of weather, don't you have trucks to pull out of ditches with that wrecker of yours?"

"Yes," the constable said. "I should be getting to the Sheriff's Office."

Fuzz, looking disgruntled, pulled on his ball cap and both men sauntered out of the diner.

"Where will you be staying?" Dixie asked. Frannie had quieted and had a pensive expression on her face as she picked at her food.

"I suppose I'll stay at Jenny's house."

Dixie nodded. "You'll be packing up her things and selling the place, then?"

"I'm not sure. I had thought of keeping it."

"Are you sure about that, hon?" Dixie asked. "If people were out to do your sister harm, then they might be willing to extend their ill-will to you."

"Or it could have been an accident like the police report said — a problem with the gas line that caused an explosion," Clara pointed out.

Frannie looked back at Dixie. "Yes, I have to agree. I'm just not sure I subscribe to your theories."

The two women exchanged a look that conveyed more meaning than words could. Both knew that the whole truth of this matter had not come out, and for Jenny's protection and theirs, just like in most conspiracy theories, they likely never would.

■ ■ ■ ■

Moments after Cord slid into the shopping center parking lot, the passenger side door to the Jeep opened and Grady Wallace got in along with a heavy swirl of snowflakes. Outside the car's windows, it was a complete white-out.

"I don't know what Plan A was, Goins, but you better skip to Plan B." He turned and looked into the back and said, "Jenny, are you back there somewhere?"

She pushed back the hood of her sweatshirt and said with a smile, "Sheriff, nice of you to join us."

To Cord, he said, "I would have been here sooner, but I thought it prudent to come in an unmarked car. So, I had to stop by my house first." He looked back at Jenny. "I don't mean to sound unkind, but you don't look well, Jenny."

She pulled the hood back up. "I suppose I'm as well as could be expected. Who knew when I exposed one of the oldest crime rings in the south, *I'd* be the one running for my life like some fugitive. How's that for irony?"

"It'll be over soon."

"I've been hearing that for awhile now."

"Could we skip the chitchat? Time's a luxury we don't have at the moment," Cord said.

"I couldn't agree more," Grady said. "Let's get Jenny over to my car."

"Wait. I wanted to suggest that I take Jenny up to my cabin, hide her there for the time being. From what I can see, the marshals that she's been with haven't done a very good job keeping her safe."

"You won't get any argument from me on that. I have to say I'm shocked that you'd suggest having anyone up at your place, though."

Cord shrugged. "It's an unusual circumstance."

Grady nodded. "That it is, but even if I was inclined to agree, there's a problem."

"What's that?"

"Have you looked out your windshield? It's a blizzard."

"Right. I still don't understand the problem."

"Roads out of town up to the mountain you live on are closed. As it is, we'll be lucky to get back to Angel Ridge. We better get moving."

Jenny said, "I can't go back to Angel Ridge. I signed an agreement when I entered WITSEC saying I wouldn't go back there."

"So she is in Witness Protection," Cord interjected.

Jenny and Grady exchanged a look. "Sorry," she said.

Grady sighed. "How much have you told him?"

"Nothing."

"I figured out she was in Witness Protection when she told me she was being guarded by marshals. Who's after her?"

"I can't answer that question," Grady said.

"It's the South's version of the mob," Jenny supplied. "I uncovered evidence that will put them away, and they want me dead. Thus, I am in witness protection."

"Jenny!"

"What? He did God only knows what to I don't know how many of them up on that mountain. They'll probably be after *him* now."

Grady gave her the look of death, but she just gave him a look of her own.

"As I was saying, Angel Ridge is the only option," Grady said. "No one's going anywhere in this snowstorm."

"Right," Cord said. "Nobody gets out either. That's a problem as well."

"Nothing to be done about weather except

wait it out," Grady said. "While we're snowed in, we'll come up with a plan to get her somewhere safe when the roads are cleared."

"Where will I stay?" Jenny asked. "Everyone thinks I'm dead."

"I'll figure that out while we're on the road. We have to get moving."

"Sheriff, I can get us up to my cabin."

"If you want to give it a go, Goins, I can't stop you, but I won't let you take Jenny. It's not safe, and I personally plan to see that she's kept safe from here on out."

"She won't be in danger," Cord said.

"I'm not taking that chance."

The two men stared each other down like two predators sizing each other up. Jenny rolled her eyes. "If you two are finished posturing, I'd suggest we get moving before we wind up waiting this weather out in a parking lot. I, for one, don't want to meet my untimely death at a Wal-Mart, of all places."

Grady shook his head and chuckled. "Glad to see your spunk's still intact, Jenny."

"Don't be condescending, Sheriff. I may be in protective custody, but that doesn't mean I suddenly lost all wit and intelligence."

"No one would ever suggest such a thing,

Jenny." Turning back to Cord, Grady said, "What's it gonna be, Goins? I can take her off your hands, and you can be on your way."

"You're off the hook, Cord. You can get your supplies and get back to your cabin to wait for spring." Jenny got to her knees and crawled toward the front in anticipation of following Grady to his vehicle.

"She can't get out of the car and walk across the parking lot. It's too open."

"It'll be fine. The parking lot's practically empty and you can barely see your hand in front of your face with all the snow," Jenny said.

"We can't assume it's safe."

"He's right," Grady said.

"Great. Perfect." Just what she needed. More men who thought they knew how to keep her safe. She had to take back her life. Maybe in Angel Ridge, in more familiar surroundings, she'd feel more herself and able to formulate a plan. Like Dixie always said, if you want something done right, do it yourself or find a woman. Luckily, she fit the bill on both counts.

Jackson checked his cell after hearing the chime indicating he'd received a text message.

"What is it?"

"The boss. Says something's up. We need to be ready to move."

"He knows where she is then?"

"I don't know. Pack up and be ready to go. Our necks are on the block. Another screw up won't be tolerated. He's made that clear."

"Right." Roy checked his gun, making sure the clip was full. He jammed it back in place and said, "Next time will be the last time. She won't get away again."

CHAPTER 6

Cord's cell phone rang; the sound of an old-fashioned telephone ringing. Jenny filed that away as a clue to what made the dark, brooding man tick.

"Hello . . . Yeah . . . No. Not familiar with it . . . Yeah . . . Are you sure it's safe? . . ."

At which point a long pause ensued. Jenny folded her arms and rotated her neck. "Want my opinion?"

That warranted a slight movement of Cord's head in her direction, but no comment.

"All right. Make sure no one follows you," Cord said then disconnected the call. Both hands on the wheel, eyes straight ahead.

"Where to, James?" The chauffeur reference wasn't funny, but it amused Jenny and she chuckled. Might as well laugh. Nothing else she could do . . . for the moment.

"Sheriff's going to meet us at the Craig farm."

"Cole Craig's place?"

"Yeah. I guess he's got an old tenant cabin and a lot of property. So, no nosey neighbors to wonder what's going on." After a pause, he added, "Grady's going to get some supplies and meet us there with the owner."

Jenny didn't comment. She wondered what it would be like to be back in Angel Ridge. Just knowing her house and friends were close by gave her a longing so acute she experienced physical pain. Lord, what she wouldn't give for a long, hot shower and home-cooked meal from Ferguson's.

She must have mumbled or moaned, because Cord asked, "You say something?"

"I'd kill for a slice of chocolate pie from Ferguson's. Don't suppose you'd stop by —"

"Not on the way, and no, I wouldn't stop anyway. It's not safe."

Just thinking about food from Ferguson's made Jenny's stomach grumble loudly. "I haven't eaten since yesterday."

"I'm sure Grady will bring food."

Jenny screwed up her mouth, imagining. "Right. Cold canned beans and meat with bottled water to wash it down. What I wouldn't give for a tall glass of cold sweet tea."

That drew a rusty chortle from Cord. "I

guess you've been away from civilization for awhile."

"Long enough to thoroughly appreciate all the things I used to take for granted," she said in all sincerity. She missed her bed, her clothes, her flat iron, moisturizer. She could go on, but it only made her more miserable, and she refused to wallow in self-pity. As they said, this too would pass. Soon, she'd be permanently relocated or returned to her old life. Either way, a sense of normalcy would return. She could endure this knowing it would end, if she managed to stay alive long enough.

Too many sobering thoughts. She needed a distraction. "Looks like it's snowing harder."

No response. Back to playing the part of the silent, mysterious stranger. Well, never let it be said she couldn't carry on a one-sided conversation. "You know, the last significant snowfall we had here was about fifteen years ago, and it fell in March. Some folks were snowed in for two weeks and more."

She'd been living in Nashville at the time and, having never seen so much snow in Tennessee, decided to drive to the Knoxville area. That's when she'd decided to move to East Tennessee. The sight of the picturesque snow on the mountains and in the foothills made her dream of making the area her home.

Convincing the *Knoxville News-Sentinel* to give her a job had been easy with her credentials, but the "good ole boys club" mindset of the old school investigative reporters on staff had been another matter. Still, she'd proven herself, working three times as hard as anyone else, and had gotten the job done with impressive results. But with precious few "real" stories coming her way, she longed to have complete control. A weekend visit to Angel Ridge and the idea had gelled.

She'd come to town to do a fluff, filler piece on the town that time seemed to have forgotten. It had been Christmas. When she arrived, she thought she'd taken a wrong turn and time-traveled into a Norman Rockwell painting complete with strolling carolers in period dress, oil burning street lamps, and horse drawn carriage tours. Carolers had been singing in the gazebo in the Town Square situated between the two sides of Main Street. There was even a bronze statue of a warrior angel to complete the picture — no soft female angel for this town. The only thing missing had been snow, which brought her back to the present.

When Candi Heart, aka Lark Hensley, had moved to town a few months ago, the sleepy little town had awakened like a slumbering dragon. Who would believe the south had its own version of the mob, much less that it was still active despite the fact that they'd closed the Vonore Gentleman's Club in the Eighties.

Clearly, a remnant still remained that had been called into duty to keep Jenny quiet by any means necessary. They could be anywhere and everywhere; back in the mountains, in the hollers, a business owner, or neighbor. It could take two lifetimes to flush them all out. She chewed on her thumbnail. She might never be able to safely return to her old life. So the question was, what would she do if she could no longer be Jenny Thompson, newspaper owner/editor/investigative reporter? Well, much like the fictional Scarlett, Jenny was afraid she'd have to think about that tomorrow.

The Jeep was moving slower and slower. The roads must be treacherous, even in a four-wheel drive. She hated lying prone in the back, unable to see anything but distorted sky and the heavy snow blowing past the plastic window. "Are we getting close?"

"I'm not sure. I could have missed the

turnoff. I've never seen one, but I think this qualifies as a white-out. At least there are no other cars out. I guess everyone had the good sense to get inside."

"Let's hope," Jenny agreed, thinking of the people out looking for her.

"Here we go," Cord said, and Jenny found herself holding on to anything she could find to keep from slip-sliding into another gas can or whatever it had been that had bruised her ribs earlier.

"Sorry. It came up out of nowhere."

"I'm all right." Except for now that they were off the paved road, she was bouncing around so much that she was certain her organs would be completely rearranged when they finally came to a stop.

"Get down. Cover your head."

Cord's voice had changed and a gun appeared in his hand. Jenny did as he said, but asked, "What is it?"

"I'm not sure, but keep still and quiet."

He slowed the Jeep and rolled to a stop. A blast of cold air whooshed into the car when he opened the door, then someone said, "Cord Goins? I'm Cole Craig. Grady asked me to meet you here. With visibility low, I thought I'd flag you down so you can follow me over to where you'll be stayin'."

"Much obliged."

With that, Cord got back in the Jeep. When he had the car in motion, he said, "I'm not sure how much the sheriff told him, so when we get to the house he's taking us to, you stay where you're at until I come get you."

It made sense. She didn't want to endanger herself or anyone else for that matter. "All right."

The road got rougher, if that was possible. Jenny groaned every time she went into the air and slammed back down on the cold, hard metal of the floor in the back. She was going to be black and blue, but alive and, hopefully, safe sitting by a roaring fire soon.

Cord came to a stop behind Cole Craig's truck and got out. He turned up the collar of his coat, following Craig as he motioned him into the small, clapboard structure near where they'd parked. All the while, he was scanning the clearing surrounding them, watching for movement.

The inside was sparsely furnished, but neat. A fire burning in the fireplace warmed the interior. Faded old curtains on the windows were closed.

"Where's Jenny?" Cole asked. "Does Grady have her?"

"No. She's in the back of my Jeep. I wasn't sure how much you were told."

"I don't mind telling you, it was a shock. But I'm glad she's all right. Let's get her in out of the cold."

"How about if I get her, and you stand watch here on the porch to make sure there's no one who may have followed us."

"Of course, but it's not likely anyone's out in this."

Cord pulled his gun out and extended it to Cole. "You know how to use this."

Cole took it. "Yeah."

Cord took in the tall, muscular blond man. He held the gun like he knew what to do with it; seemed trustworthy. Cord nodded and turned back for Jenny.

He unsnapped the window flap at the rear of the Jeep and let down the tailgate.

Jenny flung back the blanket covering her, sneezed several times, and rubbed her eyes. "You might want to consider laundering these things."

Leave it to a woman to worry about things being soft and sweet-smelling. Her blonde hair was half in her ponytail, the rest hung in disheveled pieces around her face. Startling dark blue eyes against her pale face were like a stomach punch. Lord, she was beautiful, even with her hair a mess, no make-up and a scrape marring her cheek.

"Let's go."

She winced as she slid towards him. "I'm moving as fast as I can considering I just got slung halfway to Georgia and back on the ride over here."

He offered a hand and when she took it, he put his arm around her back and pulled her to the edge of the tailgate. She slung her legs over, and he tried not to notice how long they were under the loose sweatpants. When she stood, she lost her balance and pitched against him, grabbing handfuls of his jacket.

"Oh . . . sorry. My legs are numb."

Cord swept her up into his arms and began moving toward the house. When she wrapped her arms tightly around his neck, all he could think of was that she felt damn good against him, and he could get used to the feel of her in his arms real easy. The last thing he needed was a meddlesome, contrary female intruding on his solitude and shattering his peace of mind. Too bad the choice had been taken from them both. There was no going back now. Feeling her warm against him, her breath soft on his neck, he was fully engaged and committed to seeing her kept safe.

CHAPTER 7

Cole held the door open for Cord, and he carried Jenny inside, lowering her to sit on the raised hearth of the fireplace. Jenny took several deep breaths and waited for the room to stop spinning. What was wrong with her? Numb legs could be easily explained, but dizziness? She lowered her head to her hand.

"Hey, are you all right? You look pale as a ghost," Cole said, coming to Jenny's side and putting his hand on her shoulder.

That's when it hit Cord that he didn't like this man putting his hands on Jenny, but since there was no reason he should have such a thought or feeling, he pushed down the urge to put a fist into Craig's face.

She was paler than she had been before, and maybe even a little green, if that were possible. "I guess it's appropriate for me to look like a ghost, since for all intents and purposes, that's what I've become." She paused, then a beautiful smile lit her face. "It's good to see you, Cole."

"I am glad to see you, too, Jenny. Don't get me wrong, but —"

The concern etching his face nearly sent Cord over the edge. "She said she hadn't eaten since yesterday," he said, trying to break the connection. "I pushed her pretty hard this morning." To Cole he said, "We hiked down Laurel Mountain."

"I'm sorry I don't have anything to eat, but Grady's bringing supplies. I think I have water in my truck."

"Thanks," Jenny said.

Cord looked around and found a cro-cheted blanket and settled it around Jenny's shoulders. She curled into it, but the bright colors only emphasized her pallor. After a moment, she glanced up at him with those blue eyes that were a surprise every time he saw them.

"I'm fine."

"The hell you are," he grumbled.

Cole came in then with the sheriff close behind. "Look who I found."

"Glad to see you all made it," Grady said.

"This is a lot of activity in this kind of weather," Cord said. "I hope no one took note and followed."

"Time'll tell. There's no other way to

know with visibility so low," Grady said.

"That's not exactly what I wanted to hear, Sheriff," Cord grumbled.

Jenny's head bobbed. She was so tired. Sleep, she thought. It seemed such a long time since she had slept. She wondered if they would notice if she dozed just for a minute. She'd probably feel better when she woke. Yes, she'd sleep . . . for just a few minutes.

Something warm and solid had her. She curled into the warmth, pressed her cheek against it. Then she was lying on something cold, but soft. After a moment, it warmed beneath her and she drifted off.

"She's exhausted," Grady said.

"Yeah. Exhausted, cold and hungry," Cord agreed. "You got supplies that need bringing in?"

"I do. Come with me." The men stepped outside and walked to the back of the sheriff's car. "Good thing about laying in this big lot of supplies is that no one suspected a thing. In weather like this, everybody was buying up everything the hardware and grocery had on the shelves."

Cord supposed that was one bright spot in this hell of a mess they'd found themselves in.

"I ran by Ferguson's and picked up some food, too. Dix had put everything she'd made for the day in 'Take Out' containers, so I grabbed three or four bags of something — I have no idea what. It's on the front seat."

"I got it," Cole said.

They took everything inside in one trip. "This place isn't used much, but it has most of the modern conveniences. Electricity and water were put in back in the Fifties. My grandparents lived here till they passed. I've kept the place up, but that's about it. I brought down a load of wood when Grady called. It's by the back door. I've got more if you run out."

Cord nodded.

"Cole," Grady said, "no one will think anything of you moving around on your own property, but if I make a bunch of trips out here, that might look suspicious. So, I'll call you, or you call me, on my cell, at home or at the station if you need to."

"There's not good cell service out here," Cole said.

"Is there a landline?"

"Just up at my house."

"I have no way to call either of you if something happens?" Cord said.

"I'll check on you as often as possible,"

Cole offered.

To Cole, Grady said, "Keep an eye out. If you see anything that seems suspicious, contact me right away."

"I don't like it," Cord added.

"Neither do I, but it's the best we can do for now," Grady said.

"Who all knows about this, Grady?" Cole asked.

"Locally? Just me and my staff. Beyond that, her immediate family. Incidentally, her sister showed up in town today."

"What's she doing here?" Cole commented.

"Probably closing up Jenny's house. I'll find out soon enough. I promised to meet with her later."

"Good luck with that," Cole said.

"Oh, and Dixie Ferguson knows, too."

"What? How did she find out?" Cole asked, then held up a hand. "Forget I asked that. Dixie knows everything."

"Right," Grady said.

The two men laughed, but Cord didn't see the humor in so many people knowing Jenny was in WITSEC.

"I guess there are a lot of agencies involved in trying to keep her safe," Cole said.

"Yeah, the U.S. Marshal Service, of course, and the Tennessee Bureau of Investigation, likely some lawyers with the Department of Justice and the Attorney General. I'm not really sure. I've been on the periphery since they took Jenny into custody. Pulling me out of the mix was the only way we could hope to maintain order in town. An old college buddy of mine works at the Bureau. I've been communicating with him. He deals with all the other agencies. I'm on a need to know basis."

Wallace would know someone at the TBI. That was a prospect Cord hadn't considered. He wondered who it was and how long they'd been with the agency . . .

"They recovered a body from the rubble of the explosion. If it wasn't Jenny, who was it?" Cole asked.

"They ran DNA comparisons from some FBI database and figured it was likely whoever set the bomb. It must have gone off prematurely."

"But they said it was Jenny."

"No. Everyone assumed it was Jenny, which worked in our favor under the circumstances."

"But these people know she's still alive because it seems they're hot on her trail."

"Of course, they know the guy they sent to set the bomb is the one who really died, but they can't exactly come forward."

"Wow."

Cord listened while Jenny slept on the couch in front of the fire, her knees bent toward her chest and her cheek cupped in her hand. Firelight looked good on her. Cord wished he could sleep so peacefully.

Cord shook his head and looked away, familiarizing himself with the interior of the cabin. It was a little more than that, really. The kitchen had all the necessary appliances. Two rooms on the other side of the central seating area must be the bedroom and a bathroom. A ladder near the fireplace led up to a loft that ran the length of the kitchen and the living room. There'd probably be another bed up there.

"We'll leave you to it then," Grady was saying to him.

"I'll check in with you tomorrow," Cole said. "You can go through all this," he nodded towards the supplies on the small table in the kitchen. "If there's anything you need, I may have it up at my house."

"Where's that?" Cord asked.

"About half a mile north of here, further back on the property. I have about eight hundred acres."

"Big piece of property."

Cole laughed. "It was bigger before we sold off part of it."

"You got protection?" Grady asked.

"A handgun with me and a rifle in the Jeep."

"Best bring it in and bolt this door."

"Will do." Cord followed the men out onto the porch. The snow hadn't slowed. At this rate, they'd have more than a foot by morning. If it stayed cold, they could be snowed in for a few weeks. Southerners weren't set up for dealing with this much snow. It'd take awhile to dig out. "While we're waiting out this weather, Sheriff, I hope you and your contacts come up with a feasible plan for keeping that woman in there safe."

"It'll be my priority."

The two men nodded at one another. As they got in their vehicles, he turned to his to get his pack, sleeping bag, and rifle. Back inside, he stowed his gear by the door and locked it, then he made sure all the windows were secure and the curtains closed. Jenny hadn't moved, so he let her sleep while he unpacked and stored all the supplies.

He found stew, cornbread, and banana pudding in the take-out bags. He located a pot, rinsed it in the sink, the set it on the stove, and then poured the stew in to warm. Jenny needed to eat. They couldn't allow her to get anymore run down. He'd wake

116

her when he had everything ready. With the food simmering, he slipped into the bathroom to take a shower.

About half an hour later, Cord carried a tray to the couch and studied Jenny's sleeping form. It had been over an hour since they'd arrived. Nighttime had fallen over the valley where the house sat. He'd brought in firewood for the night. She had to be starving.

He set the tray on a nearby table and eased himself onto the edge of the couch. Jenny didn't stir. He reached out unable to resist brushing the hair off her forehead. She was burning up. He cursed himself for making the fire too big and for not checking on her sooner. He had been sitting here for only a moment, and already he was sweating. The odd thing was that Jenny's skin was dry.

He tried to pull the blanket down from beneath her chin, but it was clinched in both her hands. Without opening her eyes, she mumbled, "Cold."

"You're burning up," Cord said and again tried to pull the blanket from her hands.

"Cold," she repeated and began to tremble.

"Okay. It's okay," Cord said as he tucked

the blanket closer around her. He left her then to retrieve a thermometer from the first aid kit he'd put away earlier.

Returning to the couch, Cord gently shook her shoulder. "Jenny? Jenny, wake up."

She stirred and groaned, but didn't wake.

"Jenny," he shook her with a bit more force. She opened her eyes, then squeezed them shut again. "Jenny, I need to take your temperature."

"Hurts," she rasped.

He slipped the thermometer under her tongue, then left her again, but only long enough to dampen a washcloth. Sitting on the edge of the sofa once more, he pressed it to her forehead. She flinched and moaned. The thermometer beeped and he removed it from her mouth. What he saw when he looked at the digital reading was unnerving. 103.

What was wrong with her? She needed a doctor, but the snow had been falling steadily all day with heavy accumulation. Her safety notwithstanding, he wasn't sure he could get her out of here even with a four-wheel drive vehicle.

Think, he said to himself. In the military, he'd received basic training in first aid, but just enough to deal with common medical emergencies.

He had to get the fever down. He went back to the bathroom to dig through the contents of the first aid kit. He got a glass of water and poured in a packet of powdered aspirin.

Back at her side, he slid a hand behind her neck and said, "Jenny, I need you to drink this." He supported her back and got her into a sitting position. When she slumped against him, he almost panicked.

He gritted his teeth against the sense of helplessness pressing in on him and cupped her head in his palm. Easing her away from his shoulder, he leaned in close to her ear. "Jenny — please. You have to drink this. Can you hear me, darlin'?"

She opened her eyes and nodded weakly.

"Good." He pressed the glass to her lips. "Try and swallow a sip of this." Cord willed her to do as he asked. He let the breath he'd been holding go when she finally took a sip. "Good girl. Try to drink some more." He tipped the glass to her lips again.

She took a bit more and pushed the glass away, her face all screwed up. "Nasty," she whispered.

"Just a little more."

She managed to down most of the medicine before refusing the rest. It was a start.

He should move her to the bed. Placing a cushion behind her, Cord eased her back against it and went to the bedroom to pull back the quilt and sheet he'd put on earlier. Back in the living room, he lifted Jenny into his arms, afghan still securely gripped in her hands. He carried her to the bed and settled her in it. She again curled into a ball on her side.

"So . . . cold . . ." Jenny complained weakly. When she began to shiver despite the warmth of the room, Cord got one of his flannel shirts for her. He eased her into a sitting position and helped her into it. The shirt dwarfed her and the dark material made her look even paler.

After tucking her in and adding an extra blanket to the bed, Cord began to pace the length of the room. She needed a doctor, but there was no way he could risk taking her anywhere.

He was able to move from one end of the room to the other in only three long strides. He'd give the medicine time to take effect and then check her temperature again. If she wasn't better, he'd decide then whether or not to go to Cole's so they could call Grady about getting a doctor over here. If someone had to come and look at her, at least they'd have the cover of night to do it in; that is if anyone could move in this much snow.

He got a chair from the kitchen and situated it close to the bed. He'd barely sat down when Jenny bolted upright in bed and looked around as if just realizing she was in a new location.

"What's wrong?"

"Sick. Sick."

He put a hand on her shoulder to keep her from getting up. "I know. Lie back —"

She covered her mouth with her hand and turned green. "Sick."

Cord grabbed a trash can just in time. He held her forehead while she threw up nothing but the water she'd drunk earlier. He wiped her mouth with the washcloth. "Would you like to rinse?"

She nodded. He supported her with an arm around her shoulders, held a glass of cool water to her lips and held the trash can up for her. He set the trash can aside and eased her back against the pillows. "Can I get you anything? I think there's some kind of soft drink in the fridge."

"No . . . Did you give me aspirin?"

"Yes."

"*Ohhh* . . . It makes me sick."

He should have thought of that. A lot of people couldn't tolerate aspirin. "I'm sorry.

Your fever is high. I thought it would help lower it."

"Acetaminophen."

Cord went to the medical supplies and came back with the bottle of pain killers. "Do you think you can keep it down?"

"Maybe."

He handed her the pills and helped hold her up so she could swallow them. "What do you think's wrong?"

After several attempts at swallowing, she finally got the pills down, then collapsed against the pillows, exhausted. "I don't know. Probably just run down, haven't been eating or sleeping on a regular schedule; been out in the cold. I'll be fine. Just need to rest."

"You should drink something so you don't get dehydrated."

She nodded, but her eyes were closed.

"If I gave you some broth, do you think you could sip it?"

"Not now. Stomach still upset. Sleep."

He pulled the blankets up around her. "Are you warm enough?"

She didn't respond because she was immediately sound asleep. He watched her carefully. She seemed to be resting peacefully, so he went to add another log to the fire. After one last look, he took the trash can to the bathroom and cleaned it out. Back in her room, he set it next to the bed.

Jenny still slept. He fixed himself a tray of food, took it to a comfortable chair by the fire and ate. This was not a scenario he had foreseen. Things were happening at a pace he wasn't used to given his lifestyle. He'd hardly had a moment to gather his thoughts.

He'd just wanted to see her safe. Now that he was alone with her, the familiar doubts pressed in making him question his ability to keep her or anyone safe. Four years ago, he'd sent an undercover team into a situation that had rapidly turned volatile. After arriving on the scene too late, he'd come away with serious injuries and nightmares from having witnessed the loss of his entire team. He should have died with them, but he'd survived to spend the rest of his life in the hell of knowing they'd paid for his mistakes.

He settled back in his chair and propped his feet on the hearth. After the weather cleared, he'd hand her over to someone qualified to deal with this type of situation. He'd return to his peaceful, solitary existence where he wasn't a danger to anyone. Until then, he'd have to turn into someone else. Someone he used to be — distant, cold, detached, unfeeling. He made a sound

that fell short of being a laugh. Not such a
stretch.

CHAPTER 8

"What do you mean you lost her?"

"The cabin came under heavy fire, sir. The marshals assigned to the detail were lost."

Jay Kennedy swiped a hand down his face. "Do they have her?"

"We don't know."

"Damn it!" He stood and paced the length of his make-shift office in the room of a budget motel in Townsend, Tennessee. "Recovery report."

"We took in a team of back-up agents as soon as we were radioed that their location had been compromised. Several assailants were killed. Our team swept the area and found nothing."

"Go on."

"The local Tennessee Highway Patrol set up a roadblock in an effort to help us find her, but they came up with nothing."

"A road— A roadblock?" Jay counseled himself to patience. "Who authorized that?"

"I did, sir."

"Did it occur to you, Special Agent Riggs, that there could have been snipers waiting for you to find her?"

"We got them all."

"You think there aren't more than those that shot up that cabin, that some of them hadn't already left when you arrived at the scene?"

"I'm sorry, sir."

"You're not just sorry. You're fired. Get out of my sight."

He turned his back on the incompetent agent and grabbed his cell to get Grady Wallace on the line.

"Wallace."

"Grady, Jay Kennedy. We have a situation, and I need your assistance."

"You talking about Jenny Thompson?"

"Yes. It would appear our agents lost her." Just saying the words made him wince.

"Yeah, I'm sorry I didn't call you sooner. I've been short on time and manpower with this blizzard and the situation on Laurel Mountain. I have her."

"What? How?"

"A local picked her up on the mountain and contacted me. With this weather settling in fast as it did, I thought it best to secure her location and then contact you."

"Tell me."

"I have her and the local who found her situated on a large farm outside of town. The farm is remote and private. With mobility limited by the storm, she should be safe there until we can figure out what the next move will be when the weather clears. Jay, if you don't mind me saying so, those marshals are completely incompetent. I'm inclined keep her out of their hands."

"Agreed, but I don't like the idea of her being in Angel Ridge."

"I know it violates WITSEC policy, but there was no other option."

"Right. Who's with her?"

"You're not going to like it."

"Name. I'll need to run a check on him."

"Cordell Goins."

Jay nearly dropped the phone. "Say again?"

"You heard me right."

Dear God . . . Cord Goins, the best field agent he'd ever seen until he crashed and burned in a covert op gone bad. He'd been holed up alone on a mountain in East Tennessee ever since. He hadn't made the connection between Cord and this Angel Ridge case. Why would he? Well, now, this could be seen as a stroke of luck or a hell of a bad situation, depending on which way he chose to look at it.

"Jenny ran into Goins by chance on Laurel Mountain. He was hiking. Look, I know it's an unusual situation, but he refused to leave her, and Jenny seemed comfortable with him."

"All right. Look, I'm in Townsend. I came in to deal with this situation personally, but got stuck. As soon as I can get out, I'll come to you."

"Right."

"Grady, I'm not sure about having her out in the middle of nowhere with Goins or anyone else," he said. "You'll need to keep a close eye on them."

"Understood. Cole Craig, the owner of the farm where they are, will keep an eye out to make sure everything's all right. I'll see that he doesn't go far from his farm until Jenny's turned over to you."

"Right. Call me on this number if there's any trouble. I'll get out there as soon as I can."

Jay disconnected the call and tossed his phone onto the bed. He walked over to the window and pulled back the curtain. Snow fell steady and hard in the glow of the parking area lights. He ran his fingertips over the bump on his nose remembering the day Cord had broken it. It had been the last time they'd spoken — the day Cord had turned in his badge.

Cord must have dozed, but he woke instantly when he heard Jenny thrashing around, tangled in the blankets. With only the fire for light, it was difficult to see what she was doing.

He moved to the bed and turned on the bedside lamp. Jenny had sat up in bed and was pulling his flannel shirt over her head, revealing a generous amount of skin.

He grasped her wrists. "*Whoa!* What are you doing?"

She squirmed out of his grasp. "Hot."

Her soaked t-shirt clearly outlined her body. Cord swallowed hard and drew his eyes up to hers. They were red-rimmed and purple stains beneath marred her pale complexion. Her hair lay damp against her forehead.

She fell back against the pillows and began wiggling out of her sweatpants. He grasped her wrists again to prevent her from taking off anymore clothing.

"Jenny, stop. Here, get back under the covers."

He pulled the blankets back up around her shoulders, but when he turned to reach for the washcloth to bathe her face, she flung the covers back and was working at removing the pants again.

"Jenny, stop!"

"Bossy men," she mumbled, then she surprised him by fighting like a wildcat. He hated to do it, but he forced her back against the pillows.

"Shh . . ." Thinking to check her temperature, with his head next to her ear, he pressed his cheek to hers. It felt moist and warm.

"Please," she pleaded. "I'm so hot."

Her voice sounded hoarse and like she was congested. "Here." He lifted the glass of cold ginger ale he had poured earlier to her lips. "Drink this."

She wrapped her hand around his and the glass. She drank its entire contents. Cord set the glass aside and once again picked up the washcloth. She moaned, low and deep in her throat when he pressed it to her flushed cheek.

"How does that feel?"

"Like heaven."

He continued to wipe her face with the cloth. He checked the bedside clock. Three a.m. "Let's take your temperature again and get some more medicine down you."

She nodded. "Tissues first. Need to blow my nose."

He folded the washcloth and laid it across her forehead. "Be right back." At the door, he turned and said, "Promise you won't start stripping again."

She rewarded him with a fierce scowl. She was not a pleasant patient. "No tissues if you come out of those clothes," he warned.

"Tyrant."

Cord couldn't help chuckling as he walked down the hall to get the tissues and a box of cold medicine. When he returned to the bedroom, he was relieved to find her just as he'd left her. He pulled several tissues from the box and handed them to her. The inelegant sound of her blowing her nose resembled the sound a goose made. Cord grinned. Jenny tossed the tissues on the bed and grabbed more from the box.

"Don't laugh." She blew her nose again. "I'm sick."

Cord tried to pull his mouth back into a straight line. "Sorry." She called him a name that he'd never heard a lady use. "Testy."

"Don't —"

Cord held up his hands in defeat. "Okay. You win. Sorry."

She blew several more times and then lay back against the pillows exhausted. Cord stuck the thermometer under her tongue and eyed the used tissues littering the bed.

He weighed the wisdom of using a kitchen utensil to get them into the wastebasket. As if reading his mind, she gathered the tissues and held them out. He positioned the wastebasket under her hands, and she dropped them in.

"Men can be so helpless."

The thermometer beeped. Ignoring her comment, he removed it and looked at the reading. *101.* "Down two degrees. Your fever's broken."

She pulled her damp shirt away from her skin and said, "Ya think?"

"Sarcasm doesn't suit you."

"Really? It's served me well until now. And by the way, I'm guessing you wouldn't be too happy either if you were forced to wear wet clothes and lie under six hundred blankets."

"Take these." He pressed two pills into her hand.

"I need a decongestant."

She was impossible! He took a deep breath and blew it out slowly. "They're cold pills."

Cord eased an arm behind her shoulders and lifted her up, then held a water glass to her lips. She popped both pills into her mouth, which gave him a moment's concern given the fact that he thought she'd never get the pain pills down that he'd given her earlier. To his relief, she swallowed these with much more ease.

"Feeling better?"

"I feel like hell and I want these wet clothes off and I need to use the bathroom."

Cord smiled again. She must feel better. "Anything else?"

"Yes. A bath would be lovely."

He pulled the covers back. Her damp t-shirt clung to her body, leaving little to the imagination. He hated himself for the feeling of awareness that coursed through him. She was ill, for heaven's sake!

He closed his eyes and lifted her into his arms. She surprised him by not protesting. Rather, she weakly rested her head against his shoulder. His heart constricted as he looked down at her. What the hell was the matter with him? He wasn't the kind of man who went all soft over women, even if they were gorgeous and vulnerable. In his former line of work, he'd seen his share. So why did Jenny have this effect on him?

It only took a few steps to reach the bathroom. "You can't take a bath."

"Please. I'm so sticky."

He lowered her feet to the tile floor, but kept an arm firmly about her waist. "You're too weak. So, unless you want me to get in there with you to make sure you don't drown . . ."

Her gaze traveled leisurely from his face to his toes and back. "Interesting suggestion."

Ignoring that, he threw the washcloth into the sink. "Can you stand alone?"

"Maybe."

She didn't seem too confident. "Just take it slow." He guided her over to the toilet and lifted the lid. He untied the drawstring on her sweatpants and let them fall, revealing brief blush-colored lace panties. Cord clenched his jaw and looked away.

"Hang onto the counter so you don't fall when you sit." He turned his back to give her some privacy, but didn't leave the room.

"*Um,* would you wait outside if I promise to stay out of the shower?"

He looked over his shoulder, his traitorous eyes going straight to her long bare legs. He turned and went out, shutting the door behind him.

When he heard the flush, he turned and knocked on the door. "Can I come in?"

"Yes, please."

As soon as he opened the door, he saw her standing there leaning against the vanity. She swayed and grasped the edge of the counter with both hands. He was by her side

134

in an instant, wrapping his arm around her waist. She grabbed his shirt and leaned heavily against him.

"Are you okay?"

"Give me a minute."

He held her securely in his arms, her face pressed to his chest. After a moment, he asked, "Do you feel up to changing?"

"Can I sit?"

He lifted her and carried her back to bed.

"I want to change. It's just that I feel so weak."

"It's all right." But she shivered, and he knew he had to get her out of that wet shirt and into something dry and warm.

He went back to the bathroom, got a fresh washcloth and ran it under the tap, then got one of his flannel shirts. Back in the bedroom, he put the wet cloth on the edge of the trashcan and sat next to her on the bed. He lifted her, pressed her to his chest and grasped the hem of her t-shirt. She offered no protest when he pulled it over her head. He took the washcloth and eased it down her back, pausing to unhook her bra.

Dear God, she was so beautiful. When she tucked her face against his neck, he felt his chest tighten again and had to fight against pressing his lips to her temple. She shivered as he eased the straps off her shoulders and quickly ran the cloth down her arms, then draped the flannel shirt across her back. If they were lucky, she wouldn't remember any of this tomorrow. He wondered if he would ever forget.

"Can you put your arms into the sleeves?"

She nodded, shimmied, handed him her lacy bra, and did as he asked. She leaned back, and when she looked up at him, he saw that she held the flannel material bunched in front of her, but his body and his brain had frozen when she'd handed him the bra. He tossed the washcloth back onto the side of the garbage can and dropped the bra onto the bed. His shirt dwarfed her lean frame. "May I?"

When her eyes met his, he saw trust and . . . awareness, despite her illness. Cord bit back a curse and forced himself to focus on the task at hand. He found the buttons while she held onto his forearms. He couldn't get the shirt fastened quickly enough. When he'd finished, he helped her lie down. Her deep blue eyes never left his.

He reached for the washcloth and held it to her flushed face. She closed her eyes and tipped her chin up, exposing the long line of her neck. He eased the cloth over her chin and down her neck to the soft hollow at its base. She inhaled sharply.

He pulled his hand away from her. "What's wrong?"

"Cold."

Cord pulled the blankets up, making sure to cover her entire body. "Do you need anything?"

Jenny rolled to her side. She blinked slowly, looking up at him through ridiculously long, inky lashes. At that moment, she could have asked anything of him and he would have moved heaven and earth to see she had it. But she simply said, "Just sleep." She closed her eyes and sighed, "Thank you."

It wasn't until her breathing became steady and regular that he could breathe normally again. Cord turned and propped himself against the footboard, fully committed to watching over her until he was certain she would be all right.

When Jenny woke, weak sun filtered into the windows beside the bed. A cheery fire crackled in the other room. She wondered where the marshals had taken her now. From the looks of it, she'd landed in a four-star resort. Mounds of pillows at her back, warm quilts, and a mattress that could only be described as a cloud made her consider never leaving the bed.

A tray on the bedside table held an ice-filled glass of golden liquid. Her tongue felt like a massive ball of cotton and the drink looked wonderful. If only she had the energy to roll over and get it . . .

"Good morning."

She stared at the person standing in the door. *Mmm . . .* this resort came with a beautiful man who in another time could have been an Aztec god. And it appeared that he was here to see to her needs. She smiled. A notion ripe with possibilities.

His jeans looked faded and worn, and he'd made use of only a few of the buttons on his flannel shirt. A delicious amount of smooth, dark skin lay exposed, and she took her time looking. She bit her lower lip to keep from moaning. He had incredibly wide shoulders. Long, silky black hair brushed them, and a dark beard shadowed his face, giving him an air of mystery and danger.

He moved toward her in the most provocative way, like a big, powerful panther stalking its prey. Jenny giggled. Maybe she was still asleep and dreaming.

When he reached the bed, he said, "Jenny? Are you awake?"

A frown marred his brow, but the imperfection made him look even sexier.

"Jenny?"

"You're handsome, you know. Very sexy."

He leaned down and touched her forehead with the back of his hand. It felt cool against her skin . . . which felt prickly and hot. "Where am I?"

He sat next to her on the bed and plopped a thermometer in her mouth. "On Cole Craig's farm."

That sounded promising. "Are ve 'lone?" she mumbled around the thermometer.

"Yes, we're alone. Don't you remember coming here yesterday?"

Jenny tried to think, but it hurt too much. So, she shook her head.

The thermometer beeped and he removed it. "Am I sick?"

He set it on the bedside table. "You had a high fever when we got here last night. It's still a little high."

He touched her face again. Very soothing, his touch. Jenny closed her eyes and sighed. "How do you feel?"

"My skin feels funny. Like it's sunburned."

"How's your head?"

"My nose is stopped up. I'm thirsty."

"Headache?"

"A little."

He picked up the glass she'd been eying earlier and held it up to her lips. The cool liquid slid down her throat. It felt like a waterfall springing up in a desert. See. He was a god. A very handsome, very sexy god.

"Are you hungry?"

She shook her head. When he would have taken the glass away, she snagged his arm and pressed it to the side of her face. *"Mmm . . ."* His soft shirt had gaped open and she had a strong urge to slide her hand inside to test the texture of his skin. A long silver chain sparkled in the light and then disappeared behind the shirt. She took another sip of the ambrosia.

"Do you need me to help you into the bathroom?"

She shook her head. "I'm good." She traced the edge of his shirt from the collar to the first button with the tip of her fingernail. A smile pulled at the corner of his mouth.

"Do you know who I am?"

She nodded. "You're here to take care of me. Like the others."

"The others?"

She frowned and felt tears burn her eyes. "They're all dead now, I think. I hope that doesn't happen to you. You're too pretty to die."

He looked so familiar. But she couldn't remember where she'd seen him before, though she was certain that she had — seen

140

him before. "Are you that actor, Keanu Reeves?"

He laughed. "No."

"You look like him." She touched his cheek, frowning. "You have scars, you know. The beard doesn't hide them."

He took her hand and tucked it under the blanket. "Rest."

Jenny shook her head. "Nope. Not sleepy. How'd you get them? Can I have some more of that?" She focused on the drink in his hand. He held it up to her lips and she drank. "That is *so* good. What is it?"

"Ginger ale."

"Tastes wonderful. So, how'd you get it?"

"It was in the supplies the sheriff brought."

"Not the drink, silly. The scars on your face." Really, couldn't he follow a sensible conversation? Maybe handsome men were like really beautiful women. Not much going on in the brains department.

"I'll get you some more medicine."

"Okay."

She watched him leave the room. He looked just as good going as he did coming. She looked around the room again. Behind her, there was old faded wallpaper with flowers on it. She rolled to the edge of the bed to look at the floor. Hardwood covered by braided rugs. She reached down to touch it. Stiff and dusty. He wasn't a very good housekeeper.

"Ow!"

"Jenny!"

The dark god rushed into the room and knelt beside her. She leaned back against the bed and rubbed the top of her head.

"What happened?"

"The floor jumped up and hit my head."

"Here." He picked her up like she weighed nothing and laid her on the cloudy bed. "You shouldn't try to get up without help. You're weak."

"Why?"

He tucked the covers around her in the nicest way. Funny he looked really mean and scary, but he was so nice, but in a dangerous, bad boy sort of way. Like Keanu Reeves in *Point Break* . . .

"You're sick."

"What's wrong with me?"

"I'm not sure."

"Do you think I should see a doctor?"

"Probably."

"Okay, then. Climb in and we'll go."

"What?"

She pulled back the covers and repeated, "Get in. I'll drive."

"Here, take these first."

He gave her two pills and held the drink up. "What's that?"

"Medicine for your fever that will help you breathe and rest."

"Oh." She took the pills from him and swallowed them. While she was at it, she drank the rest of the golden liquid. That's when she started giggling and couldn't stop. "Are you sure that wasn't ambrosia? I think maybe you're trying to get me drunk."

Another wave of giggles came. The sexy man stood and began pacing. Watching him move back and forth — back and forth — made her dizzy. She closed her eyes and pressed her palms to her temples. *"Whew . . ."*

"What's wrong?"

When she opened her eyes, he was standing over her. "I feel really weird."

He sat next to her again. "Close your eyes."

She did and he cupped her head in his hands. Then his lovely fingers began doing magical things to her temples.

"Just relax and try to rest."

"Yes, rest. I'll just take a little nap . . ."

After she fell asleep, Cord stood and began pacing the room again. She delirious. It was the fever talking. He raked a hand through his hair. He'd hoped her temperature would be down this morning but it wasn't. It was the same as when he'd taken it in the middle of the night. He didn't know what else he could do for her. He needed help.

CHAPTER 9

He checked on her one more time, then grabbed his coat. Outside, the snow was level with the porch and still coming down. He opened his phone, and he marched around in the snow until he found a spot with weak signal. Trying to stand very still, he dialed directory assistance and asked for the number of a doctor in Angel Ridge. When asked if he wanted to pay the extra to be connected, he agreed.

After two rings, a woman answered. "Doctor's office."

"Hello, my wife is ill. I was wondering if I could speak to the doctor?"

"He's out. This is his nurse. With whom am I speaking?"

"I'm from out of town. We got stuck here in the snowstorm."

"I see. What are your wife's symptoms?"

"Fever, congestion, nausea, dizziness, fatigue."

"Temperature?"

"Was 103, but it's down to 101, and it's been there since three a.m."

"How long has she been ill?

"Since yesterday afternoon."

"What have you given her?"

"Over the counter cold medication with something in it for pain and fever."

"Is the nausea persistent?"

"No. She threw up one time. She said it was a reaction to aspirin I gave her."

"Okay. Is she achy? Have a headache?"

"Yes."

"Sounds like the flu or a virus. Could be a respiratory infection. Is she coughing?"

"No."

"Good. If she had pneumonia, you'd have to get her to our office which would be difficult right now."

"Right."

"Is she able to keep fluids down?"

"Yes."

"Good. Give her as much as she'll take. She's probably a bit dehydrated and that could prevent her fever from coming down."

"Does she need antibiotics?"

"That's hard to say. If it's the flu or a virus, it'll run its course. If it's a respiratory infection, then she would need them. But since she has a high fever, we'll rule it out unless you can't get the fever down."

Cord gritted his teeth. He hated feeling helpless. "And if I can't get the fever down?"

"Call me back tomorrow and we'll try to get the doctor to you."

"All right. Thank you."

When he disconnected the call, he had the urge to crush the phone in his hand and throw it as far as he could. The nurse had told him to wait. Two things that he was not: patient or good in situations he couldn't control. He turned back toward the house knowing he'd have to do what the nurse had said — wait it out — and there was nothing he could do about it.

Grady checked the caller ID on his cell and said, "Fuzz, I been meaning to call you."

"Reckon I saved you the trouble, then. Hey, I just wanted to let you know I was out in the wrecker with the plow on the front, trying to keep the main roads cleared, and noticed something strange."

"What's that?"

"Looks like there's smoke coming out of the chimney at that old tenant cabin on the Craig farm."

"Yeah, I wish I'd had the chance to check in with you sooner, but it's been crazy around here with this storm. I need you to help me keep an eye out for any outsiders that may have gotten stuck in town because of the snow. There was a situation up on Laurel Mountain last night."

"You don't say."

"Yeah, the Marshal Service, in their wisdom, decided to hide Jenny Thompson in a cabin up there."

"What?"

"Yeah, some backwoods boys found them and shot the place up. We suspect it was part of the crime ring she busted last fall."

"Sorry to hear that. I hope everybody's okay."

"Well, Jenny got out, but the marshals didn't fare so well."

"Where is she now?"

"We got her up at the Craig farm in that tenant house."

"That explains it then. I thought maybe some hunters had got stuck out in this and helped themselves to the shelter." He paused, then added, "I sure am glad to know Jenny's all right. Who's with her?"

"A local and Cole."

"All right, well, I'll keep a lookout and let you know if I see anything unusual."

"I appreciate that, Fuzz."

Fuzz disconnected the call, and smiling, placed another.

"Yeah, boss."

"Have you found the girl yet?" he asked, knowing the answer.

"We been lookin', but —"

"Shut up and listen, you idiot. She's out at the Craig farm, about five miles outside of Angel Ridge. Retrieve her."

"That might be difficult in this weather."

He ground his teeth. "You're paid well to deal with any situation, so I don't care how difficult it is."

"There's a blizzard in the area, boss."

"I'm aware of the weather, stupid."

"But it's so far from any main roads, snow plows won't get out that way for awhile and the elevation will mean deeper snow."

"I'm plowing the road where she is now, so stop with the excuses. Take every available man. Use any means necessary. She needs to be eliminated by morning."

Cord scanned the property and the woods at the perimeter. When he saw no movement or activity, he went back inside the house. Jenny stood in the kitchen wearing only his green flannel shirt and a confused look. She had a glass in her hand.

"Hello."

"Hi." Standing there in his shirt, she looked as sexy as she would have in a lacy, low-cut negligee. She still had the confused look, but seemed steady on her feet. "Were you looking for something?"

"Uh-huh." She cleared her throat. "I mean, yes."

Cord took off his coat and hung it on one of the pegs by the door. He moved into the room, watching her carefully. Her color was better. She wasn't quite as flushed. "Did you want something to drink?"

She looked at the empty glass in her hand. "Yes. Yes, that was it." She ran a hand through her tousled hair. "I'm sorry. I'm having trouble putting thoughts together."

She walked over to the refrigerator, opened the freezer and frowned.

He came up behind her, reached in and grabbed a handful of ice which he transferred to her glass.

"Thanks."

"You're welcome." He got a ginger ale out of the refrigerator, unscrewed the cap and poured it in her glass.

"I'm not helpless," she complained weakly.

"Of course you're not."

She walked over to the small table and sat. He wanted to touch her face to check her temperature, but wasn't sure of her present mood. So instead, he asked, "How's your temperature?"

"101."

"Maybe you should get back in bed."

"I was looking for my pants before I came in here to . . ."

"Get something to drink?" he supplied.

"Yes."

"Your pants are in the bathroom drying. Last night, I rinsed them out and hung them over the shower rod."

She nodded. "Oh. Thank you."

"I'll bring them to you when they're dry."

She nodded, then asked again, "Where are we?"

"Cole Craig's farm."

"Where is that? I've seen Cole in town, but don't know where he lives."

"You really don't remember coming here yesterday?"

"No."

"He has a farm just outside Angel Ridge."

"Are we safe? No one followed us?"

"You're safe. There's no one out here but us and Cole."

She looked around. "He's here, too?"

He almost laughed. She was really disoriented. "Not here. This is a house on his property. He's up at his house."

"Oh."

This was better than earlier when she'd been talking out of her head . . . and coming on to him. Any improvement was good. He'd take it.

She sipped her soft drink in silence. "Can I get you some toast or juice?"

She thought about that for a moment. "Sure."

He got up and put bread in the toaster, then got a glass from the cabinet and poured orange juice in it. "Would you like anything on the toast?"

"A little honey?"

He went to the pantry to get the honey, and spooned it onto the bread when it was ready. He placed the plate and juice in front of her, then went into the living room, got an afghan, brought it back and tucked it around her stunning legs.

"Thanks."

She nibbled on the toast and drank most of the juice. When she'd gotten one triangle down, she pushed the plate aside. "I can't eat any more."

He nodded, trying not to watch as she licked the sticky honey off her fingers. "Would you like to go back to bed now? Or maybe you'd like to lie on the couch and look out at the meadow."

"That sounds nice."

He took her elbow and helped her stand. She deliberately stepped away from his touch and preceded him into the adjacent room with the blanket thrown over her arm and trailing behind her. He followed closely, looking for any signs of weakness. He didn't want her falling and injuring herself.

"Wow." She stopped moving when she got a look at the view from the windows. "I've never seen so much snow. It's really coming down."

"It started yesterday afternoon."

"How much is there?"

"At least a foot. Maybe more."

"Really?"

She walked over to the window, touched her fingertips to the glass. "Is it very cold?"

"About thirty degrees."

"Beautiful," she breathed.

"Come away from the window. You'll still be able to see from the couch."

"And no one will be able to see me from there?"

"Right.

She took a deep breath and exhaled. She looked over her shoulder at the couch as if it were too far away. Cord slipped an arm around her waist. She leaned heavily against him as they walked back across the room.

"Sorry. I'm just a little weak."

"You've been pretty sick." He piled up pillows at the end of the sofa. She lay back against them pulling the afghan up around her. "Can I get you another blanket?"

"No, thank you."

Cord went back to the kitchen and fixed her another drink. When he returned to the living room, she was sound asleep. He set the drink on a nearby table within easy reach, then went to the bedroom, and stripped the sheets from the bed. After he'd put on fresh ones, he took the others to kitchen and put them in a plastic bag.

Relief settled over him now that she seemed better. He just hoped her temperature would come down and that there wouldn't be any further complications. Then he could get her up to his cabin.

CHAPTER 10

Jenny woke feeling much better. A heavenly smell coming from the kitchen made her stomach growl. Upon investigation, she found Cord at the stove stirring something in a large pot. Steam curled out of it carrying the savory aroma. Jenny's stomach growled again. Darkening shadows outside the window meant it must be late.

"That smells wonderful."

Cord turned. He seemed surprised to see her standing there. "I didn't hear you."

"It's hard to make noise when you're shuffling around in over-sized socks." She wiggled her toes, drawing his attention to her feet, but also unintentionally to her bare legs, which he clearly liked looking at.

His gaze returned slowly to hers. "How do you feel?"

She licked her dry lips. "Hungry."

"It should be ready soon. Have a seat and I'll give you some bread."

He bent to open the oven and remove a pan of cornbread, but she said, "I think I'll freshen up first."

"Sure." He closed the oven door and put the lid back on the pot. "Do you need help?"

Tempting. Very tempting. He was wearing dark jeans and a dark green flannel shirt, again with just the middle buttons fastened. Jenny chewed on her lower lip. "I'm afraid I don't remember where the bathroom is." She wondered that she could remember her name while she was in the same room with this man. It wasn't just that he was handsome and sinfully sexy. Something about him drew her to him. Compelling. Yes, that was it. He was compelling and mysterious, reminding Jenny that she'd just begun unraveling the mystery of him when she'd gotten ill.

He joined her at the doorway to the kitchen. She pressed her back to the doorframe when he came closer. An exotic scent clung to his skin, teasing her nose. He lifted a hand to her cheek. She shivered. His touch combined with his nearness did all manner of wild things to her weakened system.

"I think your fever is down."

Really? Heat, that had nothing to do with her fever, spread from the top of her head all the way to her toes. She made an effort to not let her disappointment show when he shoved his hands into the pockets of his snug-fitting jeans.

"The bathroom's just over there, by the bedroom. Your clothes are on the counter."

Not trusting herself to speak, she nodded.

"There are towels and washcloths on the shelf over the toilet. If you need anything or if you start to feel ill and need help, just call. I'll be nearby."

Jenny somehow got herself to the bathroom and closed the door, but his promise to be close by resulted in myriad images of her naked in the shower and him coming to join her. She put a hand to her head. She must still be delirious. A fuzzy memory intruded of gentle hands caring for her last night and this morning that left a tangle of warm feelings fluttering in her stomach. She'd never allowed anyone to take care of her, not even her mother. She'd preferred her sister when she was sick. And now — no, she wouldn't go there, not unless she wanted to burst into tears, and she refused to cry right now.

She used the bathroom, then stripped out of Cord's flannel shirt. She was naked beneath it save her panties, which meant he must have gotten her that way. "Holy . . ."

She squeezed her eyes shut. This was doing nothing to get her wayward thoughts under control!

The shower would be quicker, but the tub looked so inviting. Her stomach rumbled its preference. She grabbed a towel, turned on the taps in the shower, adjusted the temperature and stepped inside. The spray of water felt like a warm, gentle rain trickling over her skin. She couldn't remember the last time she'd had the luxury of a leisurely shower.

"What are you doing?"

Jenny gasped and instinctively covered herself even though a shower curtain separated them. She wiped the water out of her eyes and stated the obvious. "I'm taking a shower."

"Not a good idea."

"Excuse me?"

She really should have checked the lock on the bathroom door.

"You're sick and weak. What if you fall?"

"I'll call for you."

"Not if you hit your head or pass out."

"I'm fine, really." She grabbed the soap and rubbed it between her palms. Cord hadn't budged. He was vigilant. A characteristic she'd become overly acquainted with since she'd been in protective custody.

158

"If I'm not out in ten minutes, you can come back and check on me."

Jenny started soaping her skin and singing a popular top forty tune. To his credit, Cord stayed put even though her singing was loud and painfully off-key. She sang louder, despite the fact that it was torture on her sore, dry throat.

After she finished lathering her body, she looked at her legs. She'd kill for a razor. If she asked for one, Cord would probably be afraid she'd require suturing afterward.

She stepped under the spray, then lathered her hair and rinsed the soap out. Short hair would be so much easier, but if she cut it, she'd need to color it. She sighed. A couple of hours at the salon, make that three to add a massage, sounded like heaven right now.

If she went back to her natural color, she'd look more like Frannie. Despite the three-year difference in their age, everyone had always thought they were twins. Again, she wondered about her sister. Had she spent any time in Angel Ridge at Jenny's house?

Probably not. It might be too hard for Frannie to be around her things. Even though they'd been close, they were very different. Jenny had been the strong one and Frannie was the nurturer. She had such a soft heart. Jenny closed her eyes. She had to focus on living her life without Frannie, but her sister had been the only true, deep emotional connection she'd ever allowed herself. That loss was nearly more than she could bear.

Trying to force thoughts of her family away, she refocused on finishing her shower. If she spent a moment too long in here, Cord, who still stood sentinel in the bathroom, would probably pull back the curtain and haul her out, naked and dripping onto the faded vinyl floor. Delicious as that fantasy might seem, it would not become a reality. She reluctantly turned off the taps.

She pulled the towel down from the shower rod and dried herself. Maybe he'd stepped into the bedroom to allow her some privacy, but just in case, she wrapped up in the oversized towel before she stepped out.

No such luck. Cord stood there, his arms crossed. His face must be thunder, because lightning flew from his eyes. She pulled the towel closer around her. "Did you need something?"

He stared at her for a moment, then took her arm and helped her out of the tub. As soon as she stood securely on the cold floor, he left the room, closing the door with a decisive click. The man definitely had control issues.

She put her bra on, trying not to imagine him taking it as well as her t-shirt and sweatpants off. She dressed in his shirt and her sweatpants, then picked up her panties and rinsed them in the sink. After she'd squeezed out the excess water, she hung them in the shower. Jenny wiped off a circle on the mirror and ran her fingers through her hair. Man, her mouth tasted like a garbage disposal.

"Cord?"

He was in the bathroom instantly. Jenny smiled. "Do you have an extra toothbrush and maybe some deodorant?"

"I put them there on the shelf."

"Oh. Sorry. Didn't see them."

"They were in the things Grady picked up yesterday."

She nodded and squeezed paste onto the toothbrush.

"Are you all right?"

"A little tired, but fine. I'll just brush my teeth, then join you in the kitchen."

Cord nodded and left the room. The man was not much of a conversationalist. She moistened the toothbrush and began brushing.

What did she expect? He lived like a hermit in the middle of absolute nowhere.

The only time he probably had to use his voice was when he went into town to shop. Heck, he'd probably found a way around talking even then. Again, she was struck by how much he reminded her of the marshals who'd been dragging her from one nondescript location to another these past months.

Those men had refused to talk to her, too. She began spinning scenarios in her mind. It was a means of amusing herself and ignoring the pitiful state of what had become her life. She'd come up with a theory on who he was, where he'd come from, and why he'd shut himself off from the world. Why his eyes were shuttered, empty and cold. Lifeless. Yes, better to focus on these things instead of his body, which was incredible, and his lips, which looked soft and warm . . .

Shaking her head, she emerged from the bathroom. "Is supper ready?"

Cord sat on the sofa, but stood to face her. "You've certainly made a rapid recovery. This morning, I thought . . ."

"What?"

"Never mind. I'll get you some soup."

He walked over to the kitchen, and Jenny noticed he wasn't wearing shoes as she followed. Was there anything sexier than a gorgeous, barefoot man in the kitchen cooking?

Focus on solving the mystery, Jenny. "It was probably just a virus."

Cord ladled soup into deep bowls, then piled rolls and cornbread onto a plate. "Where would you catch a virus?"

"Who knows? Maybe I got it from one of the marshals."

Cord sat and Jenny wasted no time on the food. She spooned some into her mouth. Chicken in a pale broth with chunky vegetables. "This is delicious. But I suppose you'd have to become a good cook to survive the way you do all alone out in the middle of nowhere." Speaking of . . . "So, tell me. What drives a man to build a cabin on a remote mountain?"

She got a look and a terse command to "Just eat."

"Is it that you're not much on talking or that you just aren't used to the sound of another's person's voice?"

The look again.

Not deterred, Jenny asked, "How long have you been up there anyway?"

"You don't need to know anything about me."

"It looks like we're going to be stuck here for awhile. I thought it might be nice if we could at least carry on a civil conversation."

163

"There's a difference between having a conversation and you trying to get me to divulge personal information, which by the way, is off limits."

"That's a pretty good vocabulary you have. Not many people from the mountains around here talk like that."

"Think what you will."

"I usually do." She took a breath. He definitely knew how to push her buttons. Sure it was a tactical move to get her angry so she wouldn't want to talk to him, but she was determined to not let him get to her. "I'm sure we have things in common."

"What would make you think that?"

"You saved my life — there's that."

"You don't owe me anything."

Jenny laughed. "And that's actually a good thing, because I couldn't give you anything even if I wanted to. I've got nothing. No money, no job, no life."

She watched him carefully. As a reporter, she'd been trained to notice even the most subtle changes in demeanor. Her statement seemed to make him a little uncomfortable. "You know, these past months, I've been in the company of more law enforcement officers that I can recount. They don't talk either."

"So?"

"So, if you don't want to answer questions about yourself, I'll have to just draw my own conclusions. Since you're a lot like them, I'm figuring you used to be one."

He pushed the bread plate toward her. "More bread?"

He was even more on guard after that statement. She'd likely hit the mark. "No, thanks. It's delicious, but I'm full." Still, she kept spooning the broth out of her soup and sipping it.

He finished his soup and went for another bowl. "There's a long history of Cherokee in this area. Are you descended from them?"

"No."

A response! Encouraged, she said, "But you are Native American, right?"

He sat and concentrated on his soup.

"Did you grow up in Cherokee, North Carolina?" she asked, before lifting the spoon to her mouth.

"Again with the two questions at once. I guess you still don't like me."

She smiled. He remembered, but didn't answer her question.

After a few moments passed, he looked up and said, "I'm here to make sure that you're safe until you're moved to another temporary location or testify, whichever comes first. Until then —"

"Until then, we're going to be alone together for awhile with nothing to do but talk." Big mistake. As soon as she said it, she immediately thought of several things they could do without talking.

"I'll find a way to keep out of your way. You can do the same —"

"It's a small house."

"It's best if we don't form any sort of attachment that will inevitably be broken."

Jenny held up a hand. "Just to clarify, do you think that I may form an attachment to you, or that you may form an attachment to me?"

"Does it matter?"

"Hell, yes it matters. Are you going to sit there and tell me that you think simply having a conversation is enough for two people to form an attachment to one another?" She smiled and added, "I do think you overestimate your charm, sir."

He threw her off-balance by smiling as well. "That's not what you were saying last night."

Trying to seem unaffected, she threw back, "A gentleman would never hold what a woman says in the throes of a fever against her."

He leaned closer and said softly, "Who said I was a gentleman?"

Jenny leaned back and blinked to clear the fog. Wait. Was he . . . "Are you teasing me?" She almost couldn't get the word out, the possibility seemed so implausible.

"About what you said and did when you were delirious? No, I'm not kidding. You were quite . . ." he rubbed his chin, searching for the right word, "uninhibited, not to mention demanding."

"Okay, stop. That may work with some of the less gullible women you've had to deal with, but I didn't just roll into town. You're trying to distract me from following my line of questioning about your background."

He looked up from his soup, but didn't comment. Just went back to eating. She smiled to herself. A worthy adversary. Excellent. Let the games begin.

"Back to your supposition. You think the Stockholm principle applies here, but I'm not your captive."

"Of course you are. You're here against your will."

"That aside, there's no way *I* would fall for *you.* On the other hand, I happen to know that men find *me* irresistible." She wasn't above a little teasing herself.

He looked back at her, surprised, and possibly amused, when she made that pronouncement.

"I noticed you checking out my legs, Mr. Goins." She sighed, turned in her chair and crossed her legs, then crossed her arms and took a drink of her ginger ale. "Yeah, it's a nuisance, guys falling at my feet. I can't tell you how many shoes I've wrecked. So, no worries. I'm used to it." She set her glass back on the table. "If you're not Cherokee, what tribe then?"

He gave her another of his looks, stood and took his dish to the sink.

"Why don't I just spin a theory? I'd say one parent wasn't from around here, your mom, and she was the one with Native American heritage. Or maybe you get your coloring from your father. He would have been from East Tennessee, but not from Angel Ridge. 'Goins' is a Melungeon name. There were a few colonies of them just east of here." She propped a foot on her chair and trailed a hand down her leg, still not looking at him. "Of course, Melungeons were often mistaken for Native Americans because of the similarities in coloring. However, researchers have found they were actually of Portuguese descent."

"Fascinating."

"Yes, but of course you'd know all that. Would you care to confirm or deny?"

"No."

"Predictable." She followed him to the sink with her dishes. "So, if you live alone on an uninhabited area of a mountain, that brings me back to why?"

He took her dishes. "I'll do these. You should rest."

"Never let it be said that I'd refuse a man who cooks and does the dishes." But rather than go lie down, Jenny leaned against the counter and watched Cord. Time to cut the crap and throw a dagger of truth just to see how it landed.

"You know, I don't remember much about last night, but I do know that every time I woke, you were there. And you were there because you were genuinely concerned. So, you can play this 'I hate people' bit if you want, but I'm not buying it."

Cord shrugged. "Suit yourself." If he'd known the woman was as tenacious as a pit bull when he'd found her . . .

"You've really perfected this bad-boy act."

He trapped Jenny against the counter with a hand at either side of her. He wasn't above using his size to intimidate. "Who says it's an act? You don't know anything about me."

CHAPTER 11

She pushed away from the counter, not backing down, and put her body wickedly close to his. "I know enough."

"How?"

"Intuition."

"Where was that intuition when you got mixed up in all this?"

"Spot on. It led me right to the bad guys."

"Who, in turn, are now trying to kill you."

"I'd do it again."

"Truth, justice, the American way and all that?"

"Right." She pressed against his chest and backed him up a step. "What about you? What made you throw away your dedication to the cause?"

"I never said I did."

"You didn't have to. A junior reporter could figure out that's exactly what you did. You don't hide it well."

She laid her hand against his cheek and

traced his scars with her thumb. He felt like she'd branded him, with her touch, her eyes.

He grasped her wrist, breaking the contact, but didn't let her go — and she didn't move away.

"When I'm following a story, my mindset is whatever happens, happens. Fear can't factor in to doing whatever's necessary to get at the truth. My guess is that you were the same way," she paused, then added, "before."

Cord dropped her hand and stepped back. Jenny followed.

"Care to comment?"

"I have to get more firewood for the night." After he'd turned the stove and oven off, he grabbed his coat from the peg by the door. "You should rest."

She folded her arms. "I'll still be here when you get back."

This was exactly why he lived alone. He didn't want to talk about "it" or anything else for that matter. He jammed his hat down on his head and stepped outside. Maybe she'd be asleep when he got back.

Jenny was exhausted. She wandered around the living room and kitchen, avoiding the couch. She almost wished they were at Cord's cabin where she could get more tangible clues about him.

She picked up the stack of newspapers and magazines lying on the table in the living room and leaned against the raised stone hearth with a pillow at her back. She opened the newspaper and scanned the headlines. A woman who had ink instead of blood running through her veins, and the headlines didn't interest her in the least. Instead, her eyes moved to the window searching for a glimpse of Cord.

Damn it . . . she'd pressed too hard, and he'd shut down. She knew better, but reason and interrogative finesse seemed to desert her where he was concerned. Physical attraction aside, she should just back off and leave him to his demons, but the need for answers was wired in her DNA. What would make a man on the run from some negative experience, likely encountered in the line of duty, take on someone like her and her problems when he could and should have turned her over to Grady and walked away? Snowstorm aside, he didn't have to be here with her. He could have left her and gone on his way, waited out the storm somewhere else. But he hadn't. Why?

She heard the back door open and close. A few seconds later, Cord came into the room carrying firewood. He walked around her and added the wood in his arms to the stack on the hearth. He didn't speak to her, didn't even look at her as he tended the fire.

"Still snowing?"

"Yeah."

"Hard?"

"Yeah."

"How much do you think we have now?"

"Couldn't say."

"A foot? Two?"

Cord shrugged.

Change of tact. "How long did I sleep?"

He added a couple of logs to the fire. "Since we got here yesterday." He brushed his hands off and set the screen back in place. "You should be in bed."

"So you said, but what you mean is anything to keep from talking to me."

"There's a difference in talking and being the subject of an investigation."

"You would know." He gave her a look, and she forced herself to take a more subtle approach. She'd handled more reluctant subjects than him. Okay, maybe not. Still . . . "I'm sorry. I can come on a little strong," she offered.

His dark gaze met hers, but rather than comment said, "How's your temperature?"

"I haven't taken it, but I feel much better."

He touched her forehead, and she felt her skin warm at the contact. Her heart rate picked up and she sighed. She — who had never sighed because of a man's effect on her — sighed. Why now when the situation was so impossible?

"You shouldn't overdo it."

"Sitting in front of the fire, reading, doesn't take much effort."

"I see you found the stuff the sheriff left for you."

Jenny folded the paper and rested it on her lap. "I haven't read a word."

"Right."

"No, really. It seemed strange to me, too, but I can't seem to concentrate."

Cord nodded and stared at the fire. The flames cast a glow over his dark skin. Jenny bit her lip. She had a crazy urge to reach out and trace the straight line of his jaw that the beard couldn't hide. She wondered what he'd look like without it.

"How'd you get the scars?" she asked again.

Cord sighed. She could see him trying to decide if he wanted to tell her or not. Waiting silently wasn't a chore. He was easy to look at.

"I got them in a . . . work accident."

"Oh." She thought maybe he'd gotten

them in a fight. Jenny set the paper and magazines aside. "What happened?"

Another pause, and then, "A window shattered."

"Ouch. How many stitches?"

"I don't know."

Jenny grinned. Any man with that kind of wound would know how many stitches he'd gotten. It hadn't been a minor injury. He'd know. "How many?"

"Twenty-three."

"That must have been painful."

"Not really."

Maybe this had something to do with why he lived like a hermit. "Was anyone else injured?" she said casually, not looking at him, but anxious to hear his response.

He turned toward her then. The wall came up, making his expression unreadable. Fair enough. She'd let it go, for now.

He sat beside her, facing the fire. For long moments, he stared at the flames and she looked at him. Tight jeans did little to hide powerful thighs and calves. He may be a hermit, but he stayed in shape.

"Have you given much thought to what will happen when you go back?" he asked.

That surprised her — that he would be interested *or* that he'd care to make conversation with her, but she was thankful he was finally speaking. She hugged her knees to her chest. "You know, I don't really worry about what's *going* to happen. Having no *control* over what happens, however, is frustrating as hell."

"I can see where that would be hard for a woman like you."

"A woman like me?"

"Independent, headstrong —"

"Why, you do know how to turn a girl's head with such pretty words, Mr. Goins."

"Confident," he added.

His gaze moved from her face to her neck, then lingered everywhere as it slid down the rest of her, all the way to her toes and back to her face. Jenny started to sweat from a heat that had nothing to do with the fire.

"Attractive."

"Careful. I'll have to issue a retraction," she teased.

He returned his attention to the fire, but not before she saw the heat in his eyes and the smile tugging at the corner of his mouth.

"I try not to think about it," she said softly.

"What?"

"What will happen after I testify."

"Haven't they told you?"

She shook her head. "They gave me some general information when I applied for WIT-SEC, but they haven't told me anything specific about the relocation or what I'll be doing when I get there."

"I'm sure you'll do all the things you did before."

Interesting. Did he know how this would work or was he just speculating? She didn't ask; just decided to let him talk. "How?"

"I'd think you'll get your new identity, and they'll find you somewhere to live and a new job. It may not be writing for a newspaper, but you might be able to still work in your field."

"Under a different name."

"Yes."

She smiled. "I have given that some thought." She smiled and rocked back and forth. "I think of it as a game where I get to reinvent myself. New name, new surroundings, new people to meet."

He rolled to face her and propped up on an elbow. He was entirely too appealing for her to be expected to think coherently.

"What have you come up with?"

"In my make-believe scenarios?"

"Yeah. What name would you choose?"

She smiled. "Well, in one scenario, the one where I'm a *femme fatale,* my name is Lola LeBlanc. Isn't that a great name? It just rolls off the tongue . . . Lola LeBlanc. I'm from New Orleans, and I have a Louisiana ac-

177

cent." She mimicked that particular brand of southern, lowering her voice. "I have a sexy occupation like running a lingerie shop or a boutique inn that caters to couples who want to get away for a romantic escape."

He cleared his throat, then sat up and leaned against the hearth next to her. "Interesting, but both those occupations would probably involve too much interaction with the general public for it to be safe."

She looked away from him, purposely trying to be coy. "Spoil sport."

"Next scenario."

She looked at him out of the corner of her eye. He seemed to be enjoying her game. Whatever it took to loosen him up a bit.

"Jane Reeves, librarian."

He laughed. "No."

"Why not?"

"You could never be quiet enough to be a librarian."

He was still laughing, but she couldn't take offense at the assessment because one — it was true; and two, she liked his laugh — a low, rolling sound that reminded her of warm honey.

"Next."

"Since you don't like anything I've come up with, what would you suggest?"

Concentration kept his face neutral as he

considered. "Christina Ray. Teacher."

She leaned back, surprised. "Explain the choices."

"The name matches your personality. Bright, intelligent, pretty."

Her breath caught in her throat. "Thank you," she said softly.

"And you could teach journalism."

She would never have chosen to teach. Even though she believed education was important, she'd always considered teaching too traditionally "female" for an occupation. She had helped with a journalism class at the high school in Angel Ridge, producing their school newsletter at *The Chronicle*. She even had allowed some of the students to write a teen page for the paper. She'd also sponsored a scholarship for the top student planning to pursue a career in journalism.

She rested her cheek against her knees. "I wonder how long it will take to get used to having another name. You know, they suggest keeping the same first name or the same initials. Seems dangerous to me to have a name similar to your old one."

"There are a lot of people in the world. You'd still be hard to track."

"Not so far."

Several moments ticked by on a clock

somewhere in the room. "You know, I think the thing that most concerns me — oh, never mind." She raked a hand through her hair, pushing it back away from her face.

"What?"

She chewed on her lower lip, then said, "I worry that in a weak moment, I'll go to my sister. I can't imagine never being in the same room with her, missing her birthday. Christmas was awful." Tears misted her eyes at the memory of spending the holiday with marshals and eating a microwaved frozen turkey dinner. No decorations. No family.

He surprised her by taking her hand and squeezing it. "It's weird at first, but you'll get used to it. The holidays become just another day."

She focused on their linked hands. "I can't imagine it. She was my one concession to being truly independent. I need her. *We* need each other. I'm not sure I can live without her."

"You'll make new friends. Start a family."

"No."

At that, he looked up at her.

"Don't look so surprised. I could never join my life to another person when I'm living a lie. Not to mention the fact that no matter where I am, the possibility will always remain that the people trying to kill me can find me and finish the job. I wouldn't endanger people I love that way."

"Not if they arrest everyone involved."

"That's not likely. The crime ring is too big and widespread for that. They may take down the main players, but there'll always be those looking for revenge and more than willing to start up where the others left off for the money."

"So you're going to live the rest of your life alone?"

She rested her chin on her knees again. Jenny had never really put words to what her life would become. Even though she'd never planned to marry, talking about living completely on her own made the future seem so dismal and meaningless. Finally, her gaze locked with his and she said, "Isn't that what you did?"

He released her hand. "We're not talking about me."

Ignoring that, she said, "Do you get lonely?" He just stared into the flames of the fire. Maybe it was the warmth at her back or the fact that she'd been so ill, but rather than filter, she said, "It makes me wonder what could possibly happen to a person to make them *choose* this kind of life."

"Some people want — need to be left

181

alone. That should be enough."

"I guess I'm just not wired that way." Feeling more lethargic, Jenny couldn't help closing her eyes.

"It's late. Why don't you turn in?"

"Okay." And she would, if only she could find the energy to stand and walk all the way to the bedroom. It was just across the room, but it seemed so far away.

Cord stood and offered his hand. She would have taken it, but she couldn't make her eyes stay open. She felt his hands at her elbows and his strength replacing her own as he pulled her up.

"Can you walk?"

She did open her eyes then, judging the distance she'd have to travel skeptically. He lifted her into his arms and carried her the short distance to the bedroom. She hooked an arm around his shoulder and pressed her cheek to his chest. He was so warm and strong, but too soon, he laid her on the bed and was pulling the covers up around her. They were a poor substitute for Cord's heat.

She looked up at him, standing there, so dark and appealing, his hands in the pockets of his jeans and she wanted him. Wanted him to lie next to her and hold her through the long, dark night; to wake up next to him in the morning. Intellectually, she knew the illness and situation were fueling these feelings. She was vulnerable. They both were in this place out of time where there was nothing but the two of them. She wondered how long before they both gave in to it.

"Can I get you anything? Something to drink?"

"No, thank you." She pulled the covers up to her chin and curled into the mattress. When he turned to go, she said, "Cord?"

He stopped and looked back at her.

"Where will you sleep?"

"On the couch."

"Let me take the couch. That can't be comfortable for you."

"I've slept in tighter spots."

"But —"

"I need to be between you and the exterior doors, Jenny."

"Oh." Good thing one of them was able to maintain focus.

He stood framed in the doorway, backlit so that she was unable to read his expression, and then he simply said, "Goodnight," and was gone.

CHAPTER 12

"I am going absolutely crazy. I want to go outside."

"No."

"Why?"

Jenny had spent the morning trying to read. When she'd failed utterly, she found a deck of playing cards and lost at solitaire half a dozen times. Cord had come and gone from the house, but hadn't told her where he went or what he did. He'd just come back in from one such excursion, and now, after rummaging in his bag, had come up with something he was spreading out across the kitchen table.

"You know why. It isn't safe. And —"

She held up a hand. "I know. I've been sick. But I'm better, and you said the sheriff placed me here because he believed no one would find us this far out on so much property."

"It isn't likely, but you shouldn't take unnecessary chances."

"I could wear your coat with the hood up."

"No."

Jenny stood and moved over to the door. She opened it and the rush of cool air made her skin tingle. She closed her eyes and took several cleansing breaths. The door clicked closed. She opened her eyes to find Cord towering over her. "Standing in the doorway is about as safe as standing in front of a window. And you don't need to get a chill."

"Yes, mother." He gave her a look, but no comment. As usual. She sighed and crossed her arms as she watched him move back to the table and sit. He looked good in a red corduroy shirt with only three pearl snaps fastened and lots of smooth, dark skin revealed. His long silky black hair hung loose around his shoulders. He pushed it back and secured it with a dark, elastic band so it wouldn't get in the way while he worked. The man was entirely too sexy for her peace of mind. She needed a distraction, badly, but trapped in this cabin, avoiding him was impossible, so Jenny joined him at the table. She plopped into a chair. He was sorting small pieces of metal and stones in front of him.

"What are you doing?"

He gave her a dark look. "Occupying myself."

Ignoring him, she touched several items on the table: silver disks and bars, different types of stones, something that looked like fishing line, and a few small tools. "What are you going to do with all this? The stones are gorgeous."

"Jenny . . ."

"Come on, Cord. I'm going crazy here. I've read everything there is to read, you won't let me go outside, and, I might add, I'm not used to being told what to do." Her voice had risen as she spoke, so she took a breath to check her growing irritation with him. "Just tell me what you're doing."

He sighed. She waited. Finally, he said, "I make jewelry."

"No, really. What is all this?"

Ignoring that, he picked up a silver disk and a hammer and started flattening it. Jenny watched, trying to digest this revelation. A jewelry maker? Cord?

"I was convinced that you had been a cop. I would have never guessed jeweler."

It frightened Cord a little that Jenny could read him so easily. If this threw her off track, then it was a good thing.

"If I let you watch, does that mean I'll have endless questions to answer?"

"Maybe a few."

He continued hammering away at the piece he'd chosen, smoothing out the edges of the silver disk.

"What are you working on?"

"A pendant."

"I noticed that you wear something on a silver chain, but I haven't gotten a good look at it. Did you make it?"

"Yes." He continued to hammer.

She edged closer. Her scent and nearness made him a little lightheaded. He wasn't sure he liked the feeling. He'd always been able to maintain control with women, but *this* woman affected him in strange ways — ways he'd never experienced.

"May I see it?"

He'd lost the thread of the conversation when she got up to stand beside him and lean in near his shoulder, but he said, "Sure," anyway. She reached inside his shirt. Shocked at the bold move, awareness pricked across his skin as he felt her hand against his bare chest. He sucked in a ragged breath, but her focus centered on the pendant she held. His pendant.

She traced its unusual pattern with the tip of her finger. "Two arrows crossed. It looks like the directions on a weather vane. You know, north, south, east and west."

"It symbolizes that everything is connected."

"And the stones in the arrows?"

"The blue is water, the red — fire. The green, earth, the clear, wind."

"And the multi-colored stone in the center? It's very unusual. It sparkles with a life of its own."

He looked away, still unnerved by nearness. "The joining of souls when two lives intersect and become one." He took the pendant from her hand and dropped it inside his shirt. Leaning forward, he began hammering again.

"Who would have known?" Humor laced her words. "You're a romantic?"

"A realist. Life springs from the joining of two people."

"Opposites attract, like water and fire."

"The elements of water, fire and wind can destroy the earth."

"Or strengthen it."

"Yes, but only when people live in harmony with the land."

"At one with the elements."

Cord nodded. She understood perfectly — all but his reason for wearing the pendant. The idealistic teenager who'd created it in his grandfather's workshop had made two; one for him and the other for the woman who would become his life mate. The second lay tarnishing in a drawer, its promise never fulfilled. Even he didn't fully understand why he still wore the pendant.

He held no illusions about finding someone to share his life. His was a life destined to be lived alone in a world where a wife's dreams couldn't be shattered by the loss of her mate. The faces of the wives who'd lost their husbands because of his mistakes came unbidden to his mind.

"May I?"

Cord looked up at Jenny, surprised to see that she was still only a touch away. She took the hammer from him. The feel of her hand against his tied his stomach in knots.

"What were you doing to this?" she asked.

"Smoothing out the edges."

She leaned over and touched the metal to get a feel for it, then hammered at the roughest spots until they felt even. "Wouldn't it be great if we could smooth out our rough edges so easily?"

He liked to think that hammering away at a piece helped him smooth out the rough edges of his ragged emotions. She might disagree.

"What type of design will this one be?"

She sat on his thigh as if it were the most natural thing in the world while she continued to work the metal. Having her so close set off a series of wild fantasies, the least of which was the urge to pull her back against him and taste the fragrant skin at the side of her neck.

She looked over her shoulder at him. "Cord?" When he didn't respond, she repeated, "What kind of design will this be?"

"I don't know." Maybe a silvery moon with dark stones that held the mystery of her — of what her life would become.

"You don't have the design sketched out anywhere?"

"No. It emerges from the metal as I work it."

She handed him the hammer. "Then you'd better take this back, because I don't know where I'm going. I don't want to mess it up."

"You couldn't. This is just preliminary shaping."

"Where did you learn to do this?"

She didn't move, so he reached around her to hold the silver with one hand and hammer with the other which resulted in settling her against his chest. It didn't escape his notice that she fit like she belonged there. "My grandfather was Navaho. He taught me. It was a marketable skill that was supposed to give me a means of supporting myself. Keep me out of trouble."

"But it didn't. Keep you out of trouble."

Cord laughed. "No." She was too insightful. He bet she was a hell of a reporter.

Jenny smiled. "Of course not." She watched him work silently for a few minutes, then asked, "Do you sell your work?"

"Yeah. I have standing orders from several jewelers and Native American galleries for whatever I make."

"Local?"

"All over."

"What do you see in this?"

He held the silver disk he'd been working on up to the light. "Beauty."

She nodded. "How will you interpret that?"

"I'll begin with these sapphires." He set aside several of the small stones. But first, he would etch out a design in the silver that would allow silvery light to flow through the pendant.

Cord moved his arm from around her so that he could concentrate on the work with a steady hand. He slipped on safety glasses and warned, "Watch out." She leaned back as tiny shards of silver flew around his hands. The curved lines were her neck and lips. The ovals, her eyes. The angled lines her nose and cheeks.

Satisfied, he blew against the surface to clear the remaining dust and fragments. Then he began putting the stones in rows beside the disc, with some deep blue topaz the color of her eyes interspersed among them.

When he placed the last stone, she said, "Perfect."

He looked up at her and agreed. "Yes."

"How will you attach the stones?" she asked softly, feeling the same awareness he did.

"I'll make settings for them and weld them onto the disk."

"Yes, then the light will flow through the silver to give the stones life."

"If the darkness from the wearer's skin doesn't kill the effect," he said, feeling his mood dip.

"Light dispels darkness."

"Darkness overshadows the light at the end of every day."

"Still, light pierces the darkness when the sun rises."

"But the two can't co-exist."

"Dawn and dusk are a mingling of the two."

"But ultimately, one overcomes the other."

The look in her eyes unnerved him. After a beat of silence, she asked, "Are we still talking about the pendant or have we moved on to something else?"

Cord grasped her waist and stood. He moved to fridge to get something to drink. He gulped down half the glass of orange juice he poured. Of course, she followed him. Before she could continue her verbal assault, he said, "Take a walk."

"What?"

"Bundle up, use my coat, don't go far." When he looked at her, she blinked, but didn't speak. Clearly, she hadn't expected him to tell her she could leave the cabin. "Go now, before I change my mind."

She took a few steps back, her eyes narrowed, her mind clearly still on their exchange. But she turned and went to the rack where his coat hung. She pulled a knit cap over her hair, slid her arms into his coat and zipped it. Next she stepped into his oversized boots. She looked like a little girl playing dress up with her daddy's clothes, a comical thought given the fact that the heat flowing between them was far from familial. She still looked sexy as hell, even with all her lines and curves concealed.

She pulled the dark hood up. Cord turned away. The door opened and closed. He didn't have to look to know she was gone; he felt her absence. Bracing against the counter, he hung his head and squeezed his eyes shut. He'd been content to be alone all these years, and now, after only a few days, she'd gotten to him. Made him feel something he didn't want to feel — something he had no business feeling for anyone. The darkness in his soul could only extinguish the light in hers.

His cell began ringing, the sound of the old-fashioned telephone shattering the silence. Surprised that he'd found a spot with signal inside, Cord pushed away from the counter and pulled the phone out of his pocket. He recognized the number even though he hadn't seen it in years.

"Hello?"

"Cord? Is that you, man?"

"Yeah. It's been a long time, Jay."

"Too long. How are you?"

Cord and Jay Kennedy had worked together at the Bureau in Nashville. Before that, they'd both been Naval intelligence officers. Jay had recruited him just after his discharge as a troubleshooting, undercover agent given the most difficult assignments. The ones everyone else had failed at and mostly in the illegal substance division.

"A witness in a high-profile case was lost on some Godforsaken mountain near you. I heard you might know something about it."

"Yeah. I'm holed up with her on a farm outside Angel Ridge."

"I'm a little surprised you didn't contact me."

"I didn't know you were involved. Sounds like a mess. Not typical for you, Kennedy."

"How'd you get tangled up in this?"

"I was on an overnight hike in the area where the marshals lost her."

"Lucky for her. I don't have a man better than you to put on the case."

"I'm not on it, Jay. You need to extract her. She's not safe here."

"No. This is good. I've talked to the sheriff, and the location where you have her will be damn near impossible to compromise."

So he'd talked to Grady. He should have known. "I'm not in the bureau anymore, Jay. I can't handle her, and you know why."

"The U.S. Attorney handling the case has prepared a motion to get her testimony moved up. She's just waiting for my call to tell her Jenny's safe. I'll contact you ASAP with the date."

"You're not hearing me. You have to retrieve her. I can't protect her here. We're in an old clapboard house a strong wind away from falling down, and it's in the middle of open farmland. The position is too vulnerable. We'd be sitting ducks if they found us."

No response.

"Jay —"

He checked the cell. No signal. "Damn it!"

He tossed the phone onto the table and raked both hands through his hair. He needed a plan for what he'd do if they were found. He walked over to the window. Jenny stood some distance away from the house making snowballs and tossing them at nothing. She looked so exposed out in the open like that. The snow came nearly to her knees and was still falling. If they couldn't get out, he had to trust no one could get in. But his mind spun scenarios where these people hiked in from the road, came by horse or snowmobile.

He'd have to stay alert until the weather broke, then he'd get Jenny out of here. At his cabin, there was a trail that led to the road from the trees behind his cabin. It would be a hard, uphill hike, but it was the best plan. They'd be much safer on the mountain. Until then, he'd have to hope that for the first time since she'd been taken into custody, their luck held and they'd go undetected.

■ ■ ■ ■

"Hey buddy, if you've got a minute I could use some directions from a local."

"Sure thing."

The man wearing a faded flannel shirt and dirty blue jeans spit a line of tobacco juice onto the pavement. Ignoring that and the smell, Jackson opened his map and held it up to the door of his utility vehicle.

"Nice ride, man. Is it one of them there Hummers like they use in the military?"

"Yeah. I'm looking for a place off this road. Craig Road. You know it?"

The man peered at the map, tilted his head to one side, then extended a dirty finger to trace a line from left to right. He scratched at a few days growth of beard. "Sure, I do. It's a few miles outside of town. Ain't nothin' on that road 'cept the Craig farm, and the roads that way won't be passable."

"Any trails for off-roading from there?"

"Naw. That's private property."

"Oh, well, anybody live out that way? Maybe I can get permission from the owner?"

Surely they weren't stupid enough to take the woman to a private residence and hide her in plain sight right here in Angel Ridge, but this was definitely where the boss had said she was.

"I wouldn't go nosin' around private property if I was you. That's good way to get shot around here."

"I'll take my chances. Would you be willing to ride out that direction to show us where the owner of the property lives?"

"Sorry, man. I can't help you."

"I'll make it worth your time." He flashed a hundred-dollar bill and the man smiled.

"Naw, man. I gotta git home to the wife and kids."

And with that, he left. Jackson watched the man hunker down and head to his four-wheel drive pickup, then looked at his watch. The parking lot of the diner was deserted, but since the woman who ran it had a room on the second level of the building, he and his men had been able to get a meal and use the bathroom. He signaled, and the boys pushed their coffee cups away and streamed out of the building.

"What'd you find out, boss?"

"Not nearly enough. Load up."

"Where we headed?"

"Huntin'."

CHAPTER 13

Grady picked up his ringing phone, saw who it was and said, "Hey, Dixie. What's up?"

"A band of the slimiest creeps I've seen in a long time just slithered outta my diner. I don't mind sayin', I didn't move far from where I keep my gun behind the lunch counter the whole time they were in here."

"Why didn't you call me sooner?"

"Don't think the thought didn't cross my mind, but —"

"But what?"

"I don't like admitting it, but I was afraid they'd get suspicious about who I might be calling, and I just wasn't up to taking my life into my own hands today."

"How many?"

"Four."

"You recognize any of them?"

"No. Grady, what the hell? You're scaring me. You don't seem at all surprised by what

I'm telling you."

"They say where they were headed?"

"They asked me about how to find Craig Road."

Grady couldn't keep his voice from escalating. He stood, put on his coat, and motioned to Woody to follow him out of the office. "Did you tell them?"

"What's going on?"

Grady ground his teeth. "Answer the question, Dixie!"

"Of course I didn't. I know better than to tell a stranger where someone lives, especially when they are so clearly up to no good. What could they want out at Cole's place?"

"What were they driving?"

"I can't help noticing that I'm answering your questions, but you aren't answering any of mine."

"I'll explain later, Dix. Just tell me." Grady got in his Jeep and Woody slid in beside him. He fired the engine and put it in gear.

"They had a dark Hummer pulling a trailer that had a couple of four-wheelers on it."

"Stay put, okay? I'm going to go check it out. You should lock up and put the 'Closed' sign on the door in case they come back. No one should be out in this weather, and anyone who is . . . well, just close up, okay? I'll check on you when I get back."

He disconnected the call. He'd pay for this later. Dixie could be relentless when something was going on she didn't know about. He dialed Cord's number. It rang funny, like there was no service, then went to voice mail. "Damn it!" He dialed Cole next.

"Hello."

"Cole, it's Grady. There's a band of men headed your way in a Hummer hauling some ATV's."

"What the hell?"

"I tried calling Cord to alert him, but he doesn't have service on his cell. We need to move Jenny."

"How are we going to move her in this weather?"

"We don't have a choice. Get down there now."

"On my way."

Cord stood at the kitchen window, watching for Jenny. When he saw Cole coming, he went to the door and held up a hand in welcome.

"Get Jenny. We gotta move her. Now!"

Cord went out to meet him. "What's happened?"

"A band of strangers were just at the diner asking for directions to get out here."

Cord's heart nearly stopped. "She's not here. I let her go out for a walk."

"Where did she go?"

"I don't know."

"Damn it, Goins, how could you let her leave the house alone?"

He went back in the house, got his rifle, put on an extra sweater and sweatshirt, then jammed his hat down on his head. There'd be time to blame himself for the critical mistake later. Outside, he scanned the clearing behind the house. "I told her not to go far." Snow fell. The hushed, white valley lay out before him.

Cord wanted to shout her name, but if anyone was out there, the sound would lead them straight to their location. He looked down at the tracks leading away from the back door. "We'll just follow her tracks. She couldn't have gone far."

He and Cole followed tracks that angled down away from the house. The sound of a creek became stronger.

"You go this way, I'm going to angle back up to the house. Maybe she wound up there."

Cord nodded and kept moving forward. "Jenny?" he said softly.

Heavy silence settled back around him. The tracks moved in both directions along the creek bank. He squinted into the heavy snow falling to see if either set ended, but the tracks were so shallow here, they'd already begun filling up with new snow. He chose the path that led farther away from the house, assuming she'd move in the opposite direction until she was ready to return.

He set out at a jog. When a large, two-story farmhouse came into view, he moved towards it. He picked up tracks again when the ground leveled off. She'd headed straight for a barn situated behind the farmhouse. When he came even with the house, Cole Craig barreled out of the front door.

"She's not here."

"I think she's in your barn."

"It's a good thing she made her way back here. Y'all were too exposed in the tenant house." He joined Cord in the yard and led him back to the barn. "Time's running out. Let's find her and get her hidden under my house."

"I'm with you on that."

As soon as they entered the barn, he saw Jenny petting a big bay horse housed in one of the stalls. Without preamble, he grabbed her arm and pulled her toward the entrance.

"Hey!"

"I told you not to go far." His hard look must have telegraphed an urgent message.

"What's wrong?"

"Some riff-raff might be coming our way," Cole said, "but don't worry. We got this."

Inside the house, Cole led the way to the back and into the kitchen. He opened a door that had a stairway leading down. "Head on into the root cellar, Jenny. Keep quiet. Cord and I will let you know when it's safe to come out."

When Cord looked at Jenny, her eyes were huge and frightened. He could practically see recent past events playing like a movie across her memory. He gently squeezed her arms. "No one's getting past me," he said, but could tell his words weren't getting through the panic that had set in. Cord grasped the back of her neck and bent so that his eyes were level with hers. "No one."

She swallowed, then nodded. He squeezed her arms again, before releasing her so she could start down the stairs to the cellar. When she turned and looked back up at him, eyes huge, he said. "I'll be back for you."

"I don't know why," she said softly, "but I believe you."

The look of trust in her soft blue eyes reminded him of others he'd failed. That was then. This time would be different. He wouldn't compromise Jenny. He'd die first.

A smile tugged at the corner of her mouth. "Don't let me down."

He nodded and closed the door.

Jenny felt her way down the dark steps and stood at the bottom, waiting for her eyes to adjust. She felt rough stones along the wall and edged her way around the cellar. She found several large burlap sacks of fragrant apples and pushing them out from the wall, huddled behind them. She pulled Cord's coat closer and waited.

Unfortunately, she had been in too many similar situations of late. She swiped at an angry tear, so sick of this — the waiting, the terror, the reality of being found that would surely come. People would die and then she'd be moved again, only for the process to repeat itself. The difference this time was she knew and cared about the people putting their lives on the line for her.

She pressed the heels of her hands to her eyes and willed the images away, of Cole and Grady lying in a pool of blood. As long as she was in Angel Ridge, everyone she cared about would be at risk.

And now there was Cord . . . he'd promised to come back for her, but she knew better. They were alike, she and Cord. Neither of them had anyone because they chose to face the world alone on their own terms. They'd both given up their lives — she unwillingly, he of his own choosing. But they'd found each other. He'd found her on the side of that mountain and saved her. Now, he could be lost forever because of her.

She punched the sack of apples she leaned against. Why? She was the kind of person who believed things happened for a reason. Why would this person be brought into her life only to die? If she were being truly honest with herself, she'd admit they had a deeper connection than she'd been willing to acknowledge, much less analyze; one she wasn't ready to have severed, but rather one she longed to explore so that she could better understand it. She'd begun to care for him in the short time they'd been together. She punched the bag of apples again. Stupid! How could she have let that happen?

Cord's thoughts shifted to the possible threat that could be headed towards them. He removed his hat, pushed his hair back and secured it with a strip of leather he kept in his pocket, then met Cole Craig in a front room. Cole stood at the window, a shotgun resting on his shoulder.

"See anything?"

"No. Nothing."

"Can they come in from behind the house?"

"There's no access. The back of the property is bordered by the river."

"Isn't it low this time of year?"

"Yeah, but it's the main channel. Too deep to cross on foot, even when they lower the lake level upstream at the dam."

"I'll keep watch from the kitchen. Call if you see anyone."

Cole nodded. "You do the same."

He checked his guns and set out ammunition on the table so he could grab it easily as needed. Then the waiting began. He stood back from the kitchen window, far enough that he could see at a wide angle but not be seen if anyone approached. There wasn't a second that he wasn't aware of Jenny waiting in the cellar below, trusting him to keep her safe.

"We got company," Cole called out. He was torn between going to see what was happening and staying put to prevent anyone from coming in the back, giving them direct access to the door leading to where Jenny hid. So, he did what he did best — let his training kick in.

"Here's how this is going to go down," Cord called out. "Wait until they're two hundred yards out, then go onto the porch and tell them they're on private property; to turn around and leave. I'll watch from here for a few minutes to make sure no one approaches from the rear. Then I'll come into the front room to back you up if needed."

"Yeah, I'm not too wild about walking out there and exposing myself to whatever fire power they're packing. Good thing Grady told me he'd have the perimeter secured, so I'm trusting that's the case. He should be right behind them to make the arrests."

Cord's estimation of the local sheriff trebled. It was a sound plan. He heard the front door open, and then Cole saying, "Hey, fellas! Y'all are on private property. You'll need to turn around and head back out to the main road."

"*Aw,* man . . . come on! We just wanted to do some four-wheeling!"

"Sorry, you'll have to find a deserted farm somewhere. This one's occupied. I'm sure you understand."

With no activity at the rear of the house, Cord jammed a chair under the knob at the back door, and eased into the hallway leading to the foyer, keeping to the wall so he wouldn't be seen through the open door.

"You got the wife and kids in there then?"

"Yeah, man," Cole lied. "Just trying to weather the storm."

"Then there's no harm in us riding the property." The speaker revved the engine of his ATV.

"Like I said, man. Private property. It's posted. No trespassing."

"Guess we missed that."

"Nevertheless, you'll have to leave. If you don't, you can be arrested for trespassing," Cole warned, his tone more stern.

"Right, like you got some big-time police force out and about in this weather."

Grady and his deputy stepped out of the tree line on either side of the house, along with about a half dozen others armed with shotguns. "As a matter of fact," Grady said, "we got a call about half an hour ago that a ragtag band of rednecks was headed this way, so we decided to come on out, in case you caused any trouble."

Cord smiled and moved back to the kitchen. The intruders were outnumbered. No way they'd open fire in this kind of situation. He set his rifle on the table and looked out the window one more time. Nothing. He pulled out a chair and sat to wait until the sheriff had these guys cleared off the property.

Thinking ahead to their next move, they'd have to relocate Jenny again. They couldn't stay here with these men having found their location. Even though no one had seen her, they had to know she was nearby with all the armed men the sheriff had brought to Cole's farm. More would be close behind. How did these guys keep finding them?

"We got 'em cuffed and will have them loaded up in our patrol cars to haul into jail soon," Grady said as he walked into the kitchen. "Where's Jenny?"

"Downstairs in the cellar."

"We have to move her. There'll be more right behind these guys. You can count on it."

"I was just thinking the same thing, but I'm a little worried about that. She's been sick."

"Sick?"

"Yeah. She's been in bed since we got here. It's just this morning that she's been up and about."

Grady pushed his western-style hat back on his head and rubbed the dark stubble on his chin. "Well, there's nothing for it. We'll have to take her into town. Probably ought to have the doc check her out, too."

"Too many people know already."

"True, but what else can we do? You'll be sitting ducks if you stay here."

"You got any theories on how they keep finding her?"

"None that I like."

Cord nodded. "An insider?"

A muscle ticked along the sheriff's clinched jaw. "Yeah."

"Who knew?"

"Everyone in my department and one, no, two other people."

"Who?"

"Jay Kennedy with the TBI."

Cord tried not to react at hearing the name.

"He called me yesterday. I told him she was with you. He wasn't crazy about the idea. For that matter, neither am I, but with this weather, we're all stuck."

"What about those men you had out there with you?"

"I rounded them up and told them I needed their help with some trespassers. They didn't know anything else."

"Who else? You said two."

"Dixie Ferguson."

"The lady that runs the diner?"

"Yeah. She found Jenny right after the explosion, but she doesn't know she's back in town now." He tugged at his hat. "Well,

211

we're burnin' daylight standing around here. Bring Jenny up and let's get her out of here."

"My Jeep's back at the tenant house."

"Right. We'll need you to move her since no one will suspect she's in a local's vehicle. I doubt they saw it when they came through. Even if they did, it was covered in snow."

"True."

"I'll stay with her while you go get it."

Cord stood, wanting to go to her and make good on his promise. "I'll bring her up."

"I can get her."

Cord tossed the sheriff his keys. "Why don't you go get my Jeep instead?"

Grady caught the keys. "Getting a little territorial, aren't you, Goins?"

He gave the sheriff a steady look. "Like you said, we're burnin' daylight."

Grady palmed the keys, then he turned and walked back to the front of the house.

CHAPTER 14

"Jenny?"

She lifted her head at the sound of Cord's voice. It had been so quiet. She hadn't even heard the door at the top of the stairs open. Light streamed in from the kitchen. Could she trust her hearing? Was Cord coming for her like he'd promised?

"Jenny?"

His voice rose with urgency this time. She came out of her hiding place and faced the man she'd hoped would come for her. Their eyes met. He took a step towards her. In that moment, something shifted inside her — something raw and visceral. She was safe, and he was here — unharmed. He'd kept her safe twice now. On the heels of that knowledge came the realization that he'd come into her life so that she could survive this ordeal. As long as she was with Cord, she'd be all right.

He stood still, backlit with his face in

shadow. He made a slight movement with his hand, like he was unsure of himself, of the strong connection she felt pulling them together. She hadn't spent a lifetime trusting her intuition to give it up now. In two long strides, she was secure in his arms.

"You're all right?" she breathed.

"Everyone's all right, but we have to go."

Her arms tightened around his neck. She'd never needed anyone besides her sister, but she knew in her core that she needed him. That they needed each other. "We?"

She felt him nod, but needed more.

"You won't leave me?"

His arms tightened around her. Jenny eased back, framing his face with her hands. Emotion softened his harsh features as his dark gaze devoured her face. She closed her eyes against the intense rush of feelings assaulting her.

"Cord?" she whispered against his cheek.

His mouth captured hers, hot and open. She met him with an intensity of her own, knowing no other way to express all that she felt for him in this moment. Jenny Thompson was not a romantic, but their bodies fit perfectly, their kiss a choreographed dance she'd waited her whole life to experience. Their bodies moved restlessly, frustrated by clothing and need.

"Everything okay down there?" Cole called from the top of the stairs.

The interruption shocked them into breaking the kiss, but they still held each other close, both unwilling to let the other go.

"Cord? Jenny?"

"Yeah," Cord said, his voice rough, husky. Sexy as hell. "She's fine. We'll be right up."

Her head fell back as Cord imprinted her neck with his kiss and they heard Cole's footsteps recede to the front of the house.

"Dear God . . ." he said.

She pulled at the leather holding his hair in place; it felt like fine silk sliding through her fingers, his kiss like fire branding her. Jenny moaned, longing for more, but knowing they had to let each other go. What a cruel twist; to finally find this when her life was no longer her own.

Jenny stepped back. Pulling herself together was not possible, but she could pretend. She looked at Cord, so dark and appealing, his desire for her evident, and she faltered. *This* was what it meant to be truly powerless.

"Jenny . . ."

He was only an arm's length away. She smiled and took his hand. "Let's go."

Cord squeezed her hand and led the way up the stairs like he wanted to put himself between her and any potential harm that might surprise them. But in the kitchen, it was empty and silent. He pulled out a chair and she sat, not because she was tired or ill, but because she didn't think her legs would hold her any longer given what she'd just experienced with Cord.

He squeezed her shoulders, like he didn't want to break contact with her. "I'll just go see —"

Cole came into the kitchen followed by Grady. Taking in Cord's hands on Jenny, his gaze skidded to hers and back to Cord's. When Cord crossed his arms, but didn't move, Grady said, "*Um,* our guests are on their way to the jail. I'll be extending our hospitality to them, and then hopefully, tomorrow, the TBI will be here when we question them. Of course, tonight, we'll offer them a deal if they turn state's evidence. Just a little something for them to sleep on."

"What about Jenny?" Cord said, but had to wait for his answer when Grady's phone began ringing.

He pulled the cell out of his pocket. "Sheriff."

Frowning, he said, "Miss Estelee? Is everything all right? . . . I'm in the middle of something. Can I call you back?"

Grady looked at Jenny, his eyebrows rising.

"Who told you that? . . . Well, as a matter of fact, I do, but — Miss Estelee? Ma'am?"

He disconnected the phone. "What was that about?" Jenny asked.

"After all these years, nothing about that woman should surprise me, but —" He broke off, staring at the phone before he pocketed it.

"What?" Jenny repeated.

"She told me to bring the folks I have, that need a place to stay, over to her place."

"You're kidding," Cord said.

Jenny, Grady and Cole all started laughing.

"I don't understand," Cord said.

"Miss Estelee is Angel Ridge's oldest resident," Jenny supplied. "She's a bit unusual in that she turns up in odd places at odd times, and, well, she seems to know what's going to happen before it happens. No one can really explain it."

"You mean like a granny woman," Cord said.

"Yeah," Cole agreed. "Like those women from the mountains that just knew things — like how to cure sickness, when a baby would be born or someone had died."

"Or when someone was coming," Jenny added.

"She's got two rooms ready," Grady said.

They all laughed again, shaking their heads.

"Good thing you're familiar with mountain ways, Goins," Cole said.

Cord nodded. Jenny fitted another piece of his puzzle in place.

"It's as safe a place as any," Grady said. "I can't imagine anyone daring to intrude on Miss Estelee. The wrath of God and a host of angels would be likely to fall on anyone who did."

"Still, you know there will be more coming in behind that bunch you just hauled off."

"Yeah. I just called our friend, Jay Kennedy, with the Bureau and asked him to contact the Highway Patrol to seal all roads leading into Angel Ridge until we can move Jenny out of here."

"That'll draw attention," Cord grumbled.

"That ship's sailed, Goins. They know she's here."

"What if *they're* already here?"

"Hopefully, that four was it. But just in case, me and the boys I brought here will be combing every square inch of Angel

Ridge tonight making sure that's not the case."

Jenny looked up at Cord. As if sensing her need for him, he turned to her. She held his gaze for a moment, trying to reassure him. "I'll be fine at Miss Estelee's as long as you're there with me." She noticed Grady and Cole exchanging a look in her peripheral vision. Cord looked at her for a long moment. She could tell something was holding him back. "You said you'd stay with me," she reminded.

He looked away from her and asked, "Sheriff, how will we get her there without drawing attention?"

"Like you said, thanks to the weather, whoever is here is here. I'll go with you to Miss Estelee's, and if anyone follows, all the better. They'll fall right into our hands. Once our guests are settled in lock up, I'll have my men come back and clear our route."

"I don't like it," Cord grumbled. "We should just stay here."

"This position is harder to secure. We'll block the south end of Ridge Road, which goes by Miss Estelee's house and leads to Main. Then we can put another block at Main and Lower Ridge Road. This way all of Ridge Road and downtown will be sealed."

"He's right," Jenny said. She looked at Grady. "When can we go?"

"As soon as Woody calls. Are you feeling okay? Cord said you'd been ill."

"I'm a little tired, but I feel much better."

"I'll call the doc to have him check you out, just the same."

"Can I get you anything?" Cole said.

Hope sprang into her chest. "Do you have Diet Coke?"

He chuckled, went to the cabinet, got a glass and then removed a two-liter bottle from the fridge and set both in front of her. She felt like a kid at Christmas! It had been so long since she'd had her favorite drink.

"Can I get you anything else? Something to eat?"

She shook her head, already uncapping the drink, and poured it into her glass. It was all she could do to keep from drinking out of the bottle while she waited for the fizz to subside. The chilled liquid hit the back of her throat and burned all the way to her stomach. The carbonation and caffeine zinged through her body. "*Mmm . . .* that is so good."

Cord looked like he'd been punched in

the stomach. Jenny frowned. What in the world?

"Cord? What's wrong?" she asked.

"We're all set," Grady said. "Let's roll."

Jenny looked at her half-filled glass longingly.

"Take the glass and the bottle with you," Cole offered.

Jenny stood, tucked the two-liter bottle in the crook of her arm and took another sip of her drink. Smiling, she said, "I feel almost human again. Let's go."

Cord took Jenny's arm and didn't release her until she was seated in his Jeep. He even buckled her in. Instead of being offended at being treated like she was helpless, she felt cared for. It was a nice feeling. "Thank you," she said as he slid in behind the wheel.

His face was set in hard lines as he started the engine and put it in gear. It was like he'd turned into another person as soon as they stepped outside. When he had moved the car out behind Grady's without comment, Jenny said, "So, you've gone quiet and intense because?"

He swung his dark gaze in her direction, still silent.

"What's with the look of death?" Guessing that he was now regretting what had happened between them, she said, "*You*

221

kissed *me.* And in case you're interested, I'm not sorry, but clearly you have feelings on the matter."

"It should have never happened."

"He speaks! Unfortunately, he speaks nonsense. And you can glare at me all you want, but it won't change anything."

"Right. Let's stick to the facts. You're a protected witness in danger. When the weather clears, you'll be moved again, and eventually, you'll be set up somewhere with a new identity to begin your new life. *That* makes that kiss a mistake. I promised to protect you, not take advantage of you."

"My situation does not preclude connections from being formed or feelings from developing. And you didn't take advantage of me. I willingly participated, in case you didn't notice."

"There are no feelings. No connection. I crossed a line, and I'm sorry."

"Have you always been this stoic or is it a new development?"

No response other than his knuckles whitening on the steering wheel.

"I'm guessing that what led you to choose the life that you have involved feeling too much. I suppose it makes it easier to live alone if you never feel anything for anyone. But now that you've allowed yourself a moment to feel something with me, it messes up your nice, ordered existence where you're in complete control."

"You should hang a shingle."

"I read people for a living, Cord. Don't fault me for being good at what I do."

He retreated back into silence. Jenny decided she'd pushed hard enough, for now. She sipped her drink as they made slow progress to town. She had another day before she'd be moved, maybe two. Cord had saved her life. She planned to do whatever she could, in the time she had left with him, to save his.

CHAPTER 15

"Come in, come in." The little woman with softly curling gray hair greeted them at the front door to her home. "I been expecting you. Come warm yourself by the potbelly stove."

Jenny couldn't help noting that Miss Estelee didn't seem at all surprised to find her alive and well.

"I can't thank you enough for taking us in." Jenny looked over at Cord who was presently scoping the place, locating exits, noting each window and making sure she wasn't standing in plain sight of them. To that end, he closed the door.

"Well, thank you, dear," Miss Estelee said to him. "I don't believe we've met. I'm Miss Estelee."

She held out her hand and Cord took it. "Cord Goins."

"Of course you are," she said. "I've seen you in town, before and after."

Jenny wondered what that meant, but half of what Miss Estelee said didn't make much sense. "Even though I shouldn't be here, it's good to be home. I just wish it was under different circumstances."

The older lady took Jenny's hand and led her into the parlor. "Now don't you worry none about that. It's all gonna turn out just fine. You'll see. Young man, take those bags upstairs. There's four bedrooms up there. Take whichever you'd like. I have a room down here, because the arthritis in my knees makes the stairs something I'd just as soon avoid. Sit, sit," she said to Jenny. "I'll get the tea."

Left alone, Jenny shrugged Cord's coat off. The small wood stove that stood in the corner of the room emitted cozy warmth. Gleaming hardwoods, throw rugs, Victorian furniture and knickknacks filled the space. On closer inspection, there were angel figurines everywhere; on the tables, in cabinets, in paintings that hung on the walls.

"Here we are."

Miss Estelee returned with a tray that held a pot, three cups, and sugar cookies. Miss Estelee's sugar cookies were legendary in town. She set the tray on a low table and poured two cups. Placing a long thin cookie on the saucer, she handed it to Jenny.

"Thank you, ma'am."

"Please. Call me Miss Estelee. Everybody does."

"I'm sorry I didn't have time to get to know you better, before. I would have liked that."

"Yes, that was you. Always running from one thing to the next. Things are a mite different now, I s'ppose."

Jenny smiled. "I prefer the running I did before to the type I'm forced to do now, I can tell you that." Jenny sipped her tea. "If you don't mind me saying, you don't seem surprised to see me."

"Why would I be?"

"There was an explosion at the newspaper. Everyone in town thinks I'm dead."

"Well, I've been away for a few months. Seems like trouble followed that newcomer, Candi Heart, into town." She lowered her voice and leaned in. "But you and I know, that's not her real name."

"No, it isn't. How did you know?"

"I knew her grandmother. Her mother, too, for that matter." The older lady shook her head. "That was a sad time when Candi's momma turned up drowned in the lake, but that one, she had a cloud hanging over her. I knew she'd come to a bad end."

"And that same trouble seems to still be

around." Jenny wondered at the need for all the research she'd done, to uncover the crime ring Candi's mom had been tied to, when all she would have had to do was talk to Miss Estelee.

The older lady patted Jenny's leg. "Honey, you did the right thing. There's evil in the world that would go unchecked if not for good people like you, strong enough to do the right thing no matter the cost."

"The costs were pretty high this time." She wondered where Cord had disappeared to.

"Give me your teacup, honey."

Thinking Miss Estelee was going to give her a refill, she took the cookie and handed the cup and saucer to her. "I'm going to show you an old parlor trick my mother taught me."

Funny, but as old as she was, Jenny couldn't imagine Miss Estelee with a mother. Still, she watched closely as the older woman turned her cup upside down in the saucer. She rotated it several times then lifted it. The loose tea leaves that had settled at the bottom of her cup formed a ring on the saucer. Miss Estelee set the cup aside and studied the leaves intently.

"I see here that you're a strong, independent woman who values truth in all areas of her life, but we already knew that." The old woman's eyes literally twinkled before she winked and continued. "You're understandably feeling that your future is uncertain, and you're worrying about that, but there's no need." She tapped the edge of the saucer. "You're going to have a long happy life, filled with love, family, and many, many wonderful friends."

Jenny couldn't help smiling. Miss Estelee was trying to take her mind off her situation by pretending to read her tea leaves. That was sweet.

"Oh, it's no trick, honey. Well, I suppose it is. I don't really have to read anything. That's just a prop so it seems like I'm pulling a rabbit out of a hat. But what I told you will come to pass. You are going to have a long happy life, and it'll begin with you finding the love of your life."

As if on cue, Cord entered the room.

"I'm always right about these things. You'll see. Now, stop worrying. You'll make wrinkles on your pretty, young face. Trust me, there's plenty of years ahead for those. You don't want to get them before your time." She leaned back in her chair, and started laughing. The sound was so sweet, Jenny couldn't help joining in. Funny, but she instantly felt better. Her spirit lighter.

"Come on over, young man. We were just having a cup of tea and some cookies."

Cord sat on the Victorian sofa opposite her, his long, lean frame looking out of place on the delicate piece of furniture. "I'm afraid I'm not much of a tea drinker."

"Well, have a cookie then."

"They're wonderful," Jenny confirmed.

"Thank you, dear," she said to Jenny. "Did you find everything you needed upstairs?" she said to Cord.

"Yes. Thank you for having us, ma'am."

Jenny was impressed. He had nice manners, not that he'd exhibited any up to now.

"Now, there's no need in you stayin' downstairs tonight to guard the door, young man. No one will bother us here."

A look of confusion etched his face. Not only could the woman presumably see into the future, she read minds as well. She was certain that was exactly what Cord had planned to do.

"I appreciate that, but —"

"No 'buts'. There's not a couch down here you'll fit on, and I'll not have any guest in my house sleeping on the floor. Now, as I was telling Jenny, my room is down here, and I avoid those stairs at all costs. My knees just won't take going up and down them anymore. So, don't worry about me wandering around up there. And my hearing's not what it used to be, either. You could run the radio or the TV all night, and I'd never know it."

Jenny and Cord exchanged surprised looks. She nearly snorted cookie out her nose! Was Miss Estelee actually implying what she thought she was? Well hell, looking at Cord and remembering their kiss, now she couldn't think of anything else . . .

"Forgive an old lady, but it's past my bedtime. There's soup on the stove if you're hungry. Help yourself and don't bother cleaning up. I'll take care of it in the morning." She stood and picked up the tea tray, but she left the plate of cookies on the coffee table. "Good night."

When they were alone, Cord asked, "What just happened?"

"I believe she told my fortune, read our minds, and gave us permission to sleep together. Did I miss anything?"

Now Cord was choking on his cookie. Jenny laughed.

"She's something."

"Yes. She does have quite a reputation in town for eccentricity. She just defies explanation. Her unexplained, *um* . . . shall we say abilities, tie in nicely with the mystical legend of the angels that are supposed to

230

watch over the town."

"Are you sayin' you think she's an angel?"

"No, I'm a bit too pragmatic. However, I wouldn't rule out the likelihood that she's on a first name basis with them and their Boss."

Cord chuckled and tried to settle back on the too small sofa.

"You find something funny?"

"The self-proclaimed 'pragmatic' newspaper reporter taken to flights of fancy."

"I wouldn't call belief in God and angels fanciful. Beyond that, there are some things for which there are no answers; Miss Estelee is one of those things."

Someone rapped on the front door. Miss Estelee, who had not yet made it to her room, opened it. "Sheriff. Come in out of the cold."

Grady came into the foyer and removed his hat. "Evenin', Miss Estelee."

"I reckon you're here to see my guests."

"I am."

She led him into the parlor. "We're just settlin' in for the night."

"I apologize for calling at such a late hour, and I won't keep you long. I just wanted to let you all know that the roads into town have been closed. There are also units placed on either end of Ridge Road that runs here in front of the house. My deputy and I will be taking turns manning a car out front here tonight."

"What about the rear of the house?" Cord asked.

"Fuzz Rhoton's house is back there. He was a security specialist in the military. I use him from time to time to help in special cases. You couldn't ask for anyone better to have your back." He looked at Miss Estelee, then at Cord. "You still have your weapon?"

Cord nodded, but Miss Estelee said, "He won't be needin' it. There won't be any violence on my property."

Grady smiled. "The legend of the angels' wings in your gingerbread trim?"

Miss Estelee pointed up. "I look to a higher power for my protection, boys."

They all exchanged looks.

"You do what you need to as far as making the town safe goes, but you needn't worry about anyone in this house. Now, if you don't mind, I was about to put these old bones to bed. Y'all stay up as long as you like, and make yourself at home."

She turned and moved down the hall, and then a door opened and shut. Ignoring Miss Estelee's assertions, Cord said, "Sheriff, I've checked the front and back door. There are no locks on either. Just the old skeleton-lock system."

Grady rubbed his chin. "Yeah, I know. She doesn't lock her doors. Never has."

His voice got louder. "And you felt this was a safe place for Jenny?"

"Yeah."

"Don't tell me you subscribe this 'angel' craziness, too."

"I've seen enough over the years to not discount it. Besides, with all these windows, there's other means of entry than the doors." He twirled his hat on his fist. "The town is secure. We've searched and haven't found anyone who doesn't belong. If we missed anything and someone does make their way to here, they won't get past us. And don't forget, you're on the inside. You'll take care of anything in here, right?"

"Right, but what if like we discussed earlier, there's someone on the inside?"

"I'll be right outside all night, and you'll be inside. If they get in, they'll have to go through us. No one is getting past me, and I know you won't let anyone get by you." Grady put his hat back on. "So, relax. Doc Prescott'll be by in the morning to check Jenny out. The TBI will also be here. They'll likely want to speak with Jenny."

Cord grunted, still clearly not happy.

"Jenny? Are you all right?"

"Yes, I'm fine." She hadn't felt safer since this ordeal had begun. "Thank you for everything, Grady."

"You're welcome." Grady opened the door. "Y'all have a good night."

Frannie Thompson swiped at the tears. Visibility was bad enough without her blubbering. Staying at Jenny's house, instead of feeling comforted, she'd felt closed in by her things, claustrophobic. She missed Jenny so much, she just wanted her back. How could she go through life knowing she was out there somewhere all alone?

A sign up ahead glowed in the darkness through the snow. Frannie slowed and pulled over. "Jimmy's Bar." Perfect. She could use a drink. In fact, getting smashed held great appeal at the moment. Anything to not feel for awhile.

The windowless metal door swung inward. The interior was dark and sparsely populated which suited Frannie fine. She sat at the bar. A thin man with a face that said it had seen more than he'd care to recount asked, "What'll you have?"

"Jack and Coke."

The man turned away to get her drink. Frannie put her purse on the bar and the folder the lawyer had given her slid out. The words "Last Will and Testament of Violet Jennings Thompson" glared at her. What a lie she was living. When the man had heard she was in town, he'd hiked through the snow to Jenny's house to bring it to her, instructing her on the probate process she wouldn't be able to begin. Another thing she'd have to discuss with the sheriff when the weather cleared. How was she supposed to deal with all this when she was still grieving for her sister?

She shoved the file back into her bag and shrugged out of her coat. Before she could unwind the long, green scarf her sister had gotten her for her birthday, her last birthday they'd ever spend together, the man returned with her drink then went back to watching the basketball game on the television that sat in the corner of the long, narrow room. No conversation. That suited her, too.

She tossed the dark straw on the wooden bar and disposed of half the beverage in one, long swallow. A man sitting four chairs down from her watched. She didn't much care; let him look. The initial burn of the whiskey was spreading a delicious warmth through her chest and lower. She downed the rest and her fingertips started to tingle. She set the heavy tumbler down with a satisfying thud. "Another." Screw the niceties. Her sister had been taken from her. There was no room for nice in her world.

The man took the glass and made her another. The other lone customer was still looking at her, so she turned to look back intending to say, "What?" but when she met his gaze, she stopped short. From the glassy look in his clear gray eyes, she'd say he'd had a few himself. He lifted his glass, took a drink, and hunkered down, forearms on the bar, his focus returned to the liquid in his glass.

At some point during the silent exchange, the bartender had brought her drink — minus the straw — and disappeared. He'd also left a bowl of pretzels. Her gaze swung back to the man with the empty eyes, but he'd forgotten about her and returned to his own personal hell. She wondered what was going on at home that prevented him from getting drunk there. Maybe he was from out of town like her. She chuckled and took another drink. She couldn't imagine why anyone would be traveling the back roads of East Tennessee in a blizzard.

He swung his gaze to hers. She looked back. He was good looking, in a disheveled, dark-whiskered, shaggy-hair-that-needed-a-trim sort of way. It fell in waves around his face. He shoved a hand into the mass and pushed it back toward his crown. He stood, stumbled, then found his balance and moved her way. She looked away and took another long draw on her drink, not sure she wanted company but nevertheless intrigued by the dark stranger whose high-end, designer clothing said he didn't fit in a dive like this. She chuckled again. She supposed she looked like she didn't fit either, but the selection of bars in the heart of the Bible belt were not wide or varied.

He sat next to her without asking her permission. His empty glass had been abandoned at his previous spot at the bar. The bartender set another in front of him without asking, making Frannie reassess. The guy must be a regular.

He swallowed half his drink, set the tumbler down on the bar and said, "What brings you to a place like this in a snowstorm?"

Frannie took a drink as well. Her whole body was warm now. "I could ask you the same question."

"If you were from around here, you'd know." He had another sip of his drink and turned back to her. He took his time looking at her. "You don't belong here."

Emboldened by the whiskey, she looked her fill of him as well. The warmth radiating to the rest of her body from her midsection shifted lower. "Where do I belong?"

They were sitting close, too close, but she noted the fact too late.

"Is this a guessing game, then?"

"I don't play games."

"Everybody plays. Not everyone wins." He swallowed the rest of his drink. "What's your name?"

She considered for a moment, then said, "Frannie."

"Nice to meet you. I'm Patrick."

He held out his hand and she looked at it, then twenty-seven years of breeding kicked in and she offered hers. His fingers were warm and well-shaped. This wasn't a man who worked with his hands. He was a professional of some sort. Maybe he was a lawyer, too. He had that air about him, like he'd stripped off a jacket and tie and left them in an expensive car before coming into the bar.

"You have nice hands," he said, still holding hers in his. He brushed his thumb across the ring she wore. Her college ring. She didn't miss his glance at her other hand to see if she wore a diamond or wedding band. "What brings you here, Frannie?" he asked, his thumb now moving back and forth across her knuckles.

Her hand felt good in his, human contact felt good after so much loss and emptiness, so she traced the lines of his palm with her fingertips. "I needed a drink."

He chuckled. "I think you had two, not that I'm counting."

She smiled. "And I'm still not drunk, so I think I need another."

He lifted his chin, looking at the bartender, taking care of her request. She brought the drink to her lips and downed it in one swallow. She resisted the urge to cough and ruin the effect.

"Impressive," he noted with a raised eyebrow. "Better?"

She smiled, but her hair fell like a curtain separating them. He pushed it back, leaving her face and neck exposed and vulnerable to him. He leaned in, his bourbon-laced breath warm on her cheek, his dark stubble not unpleasantly rough against her cheek. He sighed and nudged her ear with his nose, his warm lips caressed the lobe.

She should move away, but the whiskey and the sadness pressing on her soul interfered with Frannie's ability to act like the proper young lady her mother had raised her to be.

"Tell me to stop," he whispered, but pressed another kiss to the vulnerable spot behind her ear. He put his arm along the bar in front of her and slid the back of his fingers along her jaw until their gazes locked again. Raw pain flowed between them. They both wanted to feel something else — needed to feel anything else. So she leaned in and tasted his lips.

CHAPTER 16

"Wow. That was so good," Jenny said.

Cord and Jenny had managed to polish off half a pot of excellent chicken noodle soup and a sleeve of saltine crackers. He lifted a glass of sweet iced tea to his lips. "There's a nice claw foot tub upstairs, if you're inclined."

"Sounds good. Are you coming up?"

Was that an invitation? He looked away and concentrated on finishing his tea, sure he was reading things into her words that weren't there because he was still feeling the effects of their kiss, hours after it had happened. "You go ahead. I'll be up in a bit."

Jenny smiled. "You're going to do the dishes even though Miss Estelee said not to."

"Busted."

She stood, but stopped when she could have walked past him. She squeezed his shoulder, and he nearly came unglued — almost grasped her wrist and dragged her down into his lap so they could take up where they'd left off earlier.

"Thanks."

He didn't know what he'd been expecting her to say, but it wasn't that. "For what?"

"For staying with me."

He looked up into her eyes and understood how people got lost in emotion. Her gaze was so open and trusting as it settled on him. He knew better than to get involved with a subject. Trouble was that try as he might, he couldn't see her as anything other than a strong, beautiful, sexy woman that he wanted. Damn it, she was deep under his skin.

"Good night," he said and hoped that his implied message was getting across to her that they wouldn't see each other until the morning. But Jenny just smiled that smile that did wild things to his heart rate, then trailed her hand along his shoulder and went up the stairs.

Cord raked a hand through his hair, visions of Jenny up there in the bathroom, taking her clothes off, sliding into a bath filled with warm, steamy water . . . stroking her body with a washcloth the way he'd like to stroke her body with his hands. He shook his head and stood, taking the dishes from the table to the sink. How the hell was he going to get through the night with Jenny just down the hall?

"Boss's gonna be pissed but good when he hears we been caught, and right here in Angel Ridge of all places."

"That's the least of our worries now. We're facin' charges. I didn't bargain for goin' back to prison."

"I won't. I'll cut me a deal."

"Shut up!" Jackson said softly, silencing his men. "Trespassing will be like a pesky gnat on a judge's busy docket. The charges'll be dismissed, if it even gets that far. Besides that, the boss has got connections in this town. So just keep your mouths shut, or I'll see to it that you'll wish you had."

The dirty men hunched over their mid-sections, trying to make themselves smaller, if that was possible.

"There are more coming in behind us. Hell, it's likely they're already here. I should've waited for backup, but I never figured the sheriff here to be anything to contend with. I won't make that mistake twice."

"We need to get out of this town."

"You say somethin', Roy?" Jackson asked.

"We should have been able to take the woman on the mountain, but didn't. We sure should've been able to take her from that farm, but couldn't. It's this town. She won't be taken here or anywhere near it."

"Aw, shut up with the superstition already, Roy. We heard it all. Don't mean nothin'," one of the men said.

"Mark my words. I've lived around here long enough to know that things happen that can't be explained."

"Backwoods rednecks," Jackson grumbled. "The only problem I got is bein' saddled with all you backwoods rednecks. Now, shut up. I don't want to hear anything else from any of you."

The followers settled in their corners of the cell and drifted off to sleep. But Jackson stayed awake, trying to put Roy's warnings out of his head while he plotted their next move.

Upstairs, a sliver of light spilled into the dark hallway from the bottom of the closed bathroom door. Some tantalizing scent from Jenny's bath water teased his nose and incited wild images to flicker across the screen of his mind like an X-rated movie. He shook his head and opened a door, then leaned against its frame, eyes squeezed shut, willing the images to fade.

He sighed and pushed away without bothering with the light. He had a long, sleepless night ahead of him, but first, he stripped to his boxers and went over to open the window. The shock of cold hit him like a physical blow. Unfortunately, it did little to cool the heat in his blood.

He moved toward the bed knowing he was going to spend a restless night in it. It was an old-fashioned double, too small for him. He pulled back the covers and lay down. The old frame creaked from lack of use as he slid in and pulled the quilt up to his waist. He put a hand under his head and stared at the patterns the tall barren trees outside the window made on the wood plank ceiling. The old house creaked and groaned like it was alive, talking to the wind and snow swirling around the house, rattling the century-old windows.

How had this happened? How had he gotten himself this deep in a situation he'd sworn never to find himself in again? He'd been living in a clearing on a remote mountain for years, his demons too strong for him to subject anyone other than himself to their torture. And now, through a set of events he hadn't asked for or been able to control, he had Jenny to protect.

Sure, he'd guarded people before in his work with the military and the bureau, so he could default to that mindset easily enough. Detach and do the work. What he couldn't explain as easily was why he hadn't been able to do that with Jenny, and even more troubling were these feelings for Jenny that had him tangled up in knots.

He squeezed his eyes shut and willed his mind to go blank, but then he heard the door to the bathroom open, the squeak of the wood floors as Jenny padded down the hall. He held his breath, imagining her stopping at his closed door, weighing whether she'd open it and come in, walk over to him wearing nothing but a towel, moonlight shimmering across her damp skin. He broke out in a sweat despite the coolness of the room. Then he heard her continue down the hall, another door open and close, and then the house settled back into its night sounds. He wondered if she'd chosen the room next to his or the one across the hall —

"Stop it!" he grumbled and turned onto his side. He punched the pillow and settled his head into the indention. Half an hour or three later, he didn't know how long he'd lain there, but he felt every spring in the mattress pressing against him. He rolled to his other side to relieve the pressure, and she was there. Standing beside his bed like an apparition, so close he could reach out and touch her.

He had to be dreaming, but when he blinked, she was still there, wearing some oversized pale cotton nightgown, sleeveless and ruffled at the square neck and hem, which barely reached her knees. The style belonged to someone much older, but on Jenny it was sexy as hell with the moonlight from the window backlighting her. He held his breath, equally afraid she was real or a dream.

She tugged at the crumpled blanket as she eased in beside him. The bed creaked and dipped. When she tangled her cold, bare legs with his, he knew this wasn't a dream. His arm closed around her, pressing her close to his chest as he pulled the quilt up around them.

"You're freezing," he whispered.

She nodded, her eyes, huge and open, locked on his. He brushed her long, blonde hair back over her shoulder. Her cold hands felt like ice on his waist and then his back.

"It's cold in my room," she explained. "I couldn't sleep."

He couldn't sleep either, but then, he never slept.

"You shouldn't be here," he said as he caressed warmth into her back and arms.

"I know. I told myself that, too, but then . . ."

He sucked in a breath as she trailed a hand around his waist and up his chest to his neck. His brain was quickly detaching from the rest of his body. She eased her foot around his ankle and he bent his knee. Jenny sighed and arched her back as she sank her hand into his hair and cupped the back of his head.

"Then it all became really clear to me."

He slid his hand over her hip, down her thigh to the back of her knee, easing it up over his to his hip.

"It came to me that we're in this space — this raw space where nothing exists. I'm not lost, but not found. I'm not the person I was, or the one I'm going to be. It's like the stone in your necklace."

She held the pendant between them, caressing the center stone with her thumb. "It's this place in the middle that the elements carved out. Fire refines, water cleanses, wind brings change, and the earth anchors and nurtures life. It's a journey getting from one to the other. The place in the middle is where all's stripped away. Life begins there, strong, safe and protected in the niche the elements carve out. That's us, Cord. We're in this space between. Nothing else matters. Together, we're safe and protected here."

"Jenny —"

She held the pendant up. "You knew it when you made this all those years ago, but it took this set of circumstances for you, for us, to really understand what it means."

She pressed her lips to his, soft and warm, then broke the contact. "You feel it, too," her breath was like the wind against his mouth, changing him.

"That's why the feelings between us are so strong, so intense."

The fire sweeping through his body could only be quenched by Jenny. And her body was like the earth, anchoring him.

"We can't deny it."

She held the pendant between them as he kissed her, its form imprinting her palm like she would forever be imprinted on his heart, his mind, his body, his soul. Their lovemaking filled all the empty spaces in every aspect of his being, making Cord whole for the first time in his life.

CHAPTER 17

Jenny woke to gray light filtering into the room and Cord's arm heavy and real draped across her waist. She smiled and eased her hand from his wrist to his elbow and back again. He pulled her back, tight against him, nuzzling a spot at the base of her neck and then pressed his lips to her skin causing a shiver from that spot all the way down her spine.

"*Mmm . . .* Good morning."

His only response was a rumble deep in his throat that vibrated against the curve of her neck. She turned and looked up into his face hovering above hers. His silky black hair hung forward, and she brushed it back with both hands. She so loved the feel of it. She loved the feel of his beard, too, but couldn't help wondering how he'd look without it.

"Good morning."

The soft look in his eyes, as his gaze

caressed her face, stole her breath.

"You're here." He kissed her, then caressed her face. "I thought maybe it was a dream."

She touched his face, his beard, the scars. "I don't think I could have dreamed anything this amazing." She continued to trace the lines of his face. "You're so handsome."

He grasped her wrist and pressed his lips to the underside of it.

"And sexy."

"It's okay, you know," he said.

"What?"

"I don't need pretty words. I know what I look like."

Time to get this man refocused. "I don't know how." She trailed a slow finger along his jaw. "How long have you been hiding behind this beard?"

"Living alone, I don't worry much about what I look like."

"I have a confession."

"Mmm . . ." he trailed a hand over her hip, down her thigh to her knee. "Sounds intriguing."

"I wonder how much more handsome you'd be if your beautiful face wasn't hidden." She pressed her lips to his cheek, "How it would feel to kiss your face instead of the beard."

He dipped his head to leisurely explore the area around her ear. After several heart-stopping moments passed, he whispered, "Would you . . ." His lips moved, very slowly, from her ear to the indention at the base of her neck.

Jenny swallowed hard. "Would I?"

He leaned back and looked into her eyes again. "Would you like to shave it?"

That surprised her. "You'd let me?"

He trailed the backs of his fingers across her cheek, focused on her lips, then raised his gaze to hers. "I'd do anything for you."

Such strong emotion radiated from his dark eyes, tears filled hers. She felt it, too, but knew they couldn't share feelings. They couldn't say the words. Her situation was too tenuous, too transient.

He kissed the corners of her eyes, catching the tears before they could fall. She felt so happy, so . . . new. Like she'd been reborn. Letting her shave his beard, to her, would be like an outward sign of their transformation. Like coming out of darkness into the light.

She pressed against his shoulders so she could sit up and slide out of the bed. She picked up her nightgown and put it on.

"Is that one of Miss Estelee's nightgowns?"

"Yes." She bent and retrieved his boxers, then looked back at Cord. Words along with coherent thought deserted her. He lay there in the bed they'd shared, propped up on a forearm, leg bent with the sheet just covering his hips. Lord, he was every fantasy she would ever have for the rest of her life.

"Come back to bed," he invited, "and let me take that off. You look much better without it."

Jenny looked down at the old-fashioned white cotton gown and the red boxers she held in her hands. She tossed them to him, and finding her words said, "I'll be waiting in the bathroom, with a razor."

Somehow, she managed to turn on weakened knees and walk out of his room, down the hall, and into bathroom. She quickly relieved herself, then washed at the sink. The woman looking back at her from the mirror hardly resembled the woman she'd been yesterday. Her hair was tousled, her lips swollen and red. Everything about her seemed softer. Was this what love did? Did it transform everything about a person into something new and better?

A soft knock at the door interrupted her thoughts. She opened it to find Cord standing there in his blue jeans and nothing else. He came in, looped an arm around her waist and lifted her off her feet. When he'd finished kissing her, he set her in the hall and shut the door. A few short minutes later, she heard water running, and then he opened the door and pulled her in, closing it behind her.

He held up a razor and a can of shaving cream. "Who knew Miss Estelee would have shaving cream in the medicine cabinet up here."

Taking the items and pushing him back to the closed toilet seat, Jenny said, "She takes in boarders from time to time since there's no hotel in town. Someone must have left it behind."

Cord sat. "Lucky me." He pulled her into his lap, facing him.

"Good thing it's a small bathroom." She turned on the warm water and put a towel around his shoulders. Then, she shook the can and squirted a big puff of foam into her palm. "Are you sure about this?"

He eased his hands over her hips to her thighs and squeezed. "No, but I sure am enjoying the process."

Jenny kissed him and pushed his hair back, soothing the cream onto his cheeks and neck in circular motions. A pleasing, spicy scent filled the air around them. She moistened the razor. Eyes that had once been veiled and empty only yesterday, now looked at her filled with trust as she took the first stroke. Dark, creamy skin appeared beneath the razor as she moved from his ear to his chin. She couldn't help touching what she revealed with every stroke and smiling her pleasure.

When she moved to his other cheek and began uncovering the scars, his eyes clouded. She touched the raised pink lines with the backs of her fingers, then turned to rinse the razor. He watched her carefully, but she kept shaving his cheek, revealing more scars as she progressed. The pain he must have endured. "Where were you when it happened?"

"An office building in Nashville."

That surprised her. That he'd been in Nashville. She wondered how long ago it had been. If she had been there, too. She moved to his neck, careful to stop if he spoke. She revealed another strip of skin.

"You were a policeman?"

"Of sorts."

Jenny rinsed the razor, then pressed it to his throat again. "Did people die? People you felt — feel — responsible for?"

Cord nodded.

She finished shaving his neck, then took the towel from his shoulders and wet the edge of it. When she'd wiped all the excess shaving cream off his face and neck, she looked at him. She was right. He took her breath away. She caressed the damaged side of his face tenderly, loving him more for what she knew he'd sacrificed. "You said a window shattered."

"Yes . . . when I jumped through it."

"You don't have to tell me."

He battled within. She held him and waited.

Cord took a deep breath and let it out. "I was undercover in a company that imported coffee, roasted it, packaged it to sell. They had opened a few local coffee shops to brew and sell the product." He paused. "It was a cover for smuggling and reselling drugs."

Jenny let him talk, touching him in a way that let him know he was safe with her. His hands tightened then relaxed on her waist. "Someone involved on the outside, that I had recently met, gave me up. This person was sent to . . . get to know me."

"A woman."

He nodded and looked away. "I didn't tell her what I did. I didn't tell anyone, ever. Telling people was dangerous not just for me, but for them as well."

"But she found out."

"She knew I was working at the company.

I gave her my story, the one the agency had given me, with credentials that checked out." He shook his head. "I still don't know how she knew who I really was."

Jenny waited, knowing the hardest part to share was yet to be spoken. She wondered if he'd cared about this woman, and felt the pang of jealousy and hurt that someone he'd given a bit of his locked-up heart to would not only hurt him this way, but also endanger his life.

Cord touched the side of her face, and she looked at him. "I had a weak moment with her. It was a mistake, one that cost people their lives and left me with these scars as a reminder."

"A reminder to never let yourself care about anyone else?" she said flatly, understanding, yet angry at the betrayal he'd suffered that had ended in his shutting himself away from the world.

"A reminder never to lose focus when lives are at stake."

She nodded, getting the message. They'd had a moment. But that's all it could be. A moment. A beautiful, unforgettable moment.

She pressed her lips to his scars, unable to look in his eyes when she asked the next question. "Did you love her?"

The pause before his answer nearly killed her. "No." He cupped the back of her head until he could again look at her. Pressing his forehead to hers, he squeezed his eyes closed. "I've never felt that emotion for anyone." His kiss, long and deep and strong, conveyed the depth of his feelings for her.

When the kiss ended, Jenny couldn't stop caressing his face. "Thank you," she said.

"For what?"

"For telling me," she touched his scars again. "For letting me really see you."

His eyelids lowered, shutters against his vulnerability. "I'm repulsive."

"Stop." She squeezed his shoulders, then pressed her lips to his scars again. "These are part of the man you are, and trust me," she smiled, "you are not repulsive." She wrapped her legs around his waist and her arms around his neck, and then kissed him, thoroughly.

Several moments later, she rested her forehead against his, thinking about all he'd told her. "I'm sure you're harder on yourself than anyone else was."

He shook his head. "You don't know."

"I know all I need to. Look at me." Cord looked out the window, but not at her, his jaw locked against the demons he still battled. "You're a man that does the right thing, no matter the cost. Why else would you stay with me, making sure I'm safe when no one else could? Why would you do that when it would have been so much easier to walk away?" He looked at her then, but an emotional barrier was still there. "Tell me."

He touched her face. "I told you already. I have to live with myself. If something happened to you . . ."

She smiled. "You do realize that not just any man would have taken me on? I'm stubborn and difficult, and it appears, that many, many people want to see to it that I'm kept quiet permanently. That makes being with me dangerous."

That brought back the crooked grin that made her catch her breath. "I'm not the kind of man that shies away from danger."

"No, you're not," she sank her fingers into his hair, framing his face, "but I think you forgot that." She gave that truth time to settle before she kissed him again. When she lifted her head, his eyes were open. The man who'd let her reveal his face and shared his secret pain with her was looking back at her. And though she didn't say it, there was no way she'd bring someone she cared for into her world. Now, in this safe space between her past and her future, would be all the time they had. She intended to make a lifetime of memories to draw on in all the cold, lonely nights that lay ahead.

He eased his hands under her thighs and stood, then turned and set her on the vanity. "We should shower." The softly spoken words were filled with seductive intent. He turned on the taps in the claw foot tub. Jenny stood and went to him.

"Good morning, Miss Estelee. I hope you slept well."

Jenny pulled out a chair and sat. The older lady set a plate of delicious smelling food in front of her.

"I slept like the dead."

Thank goodness! Jenny dug into her food. "This is wonderful, Miss Estelee. I'm so hungry."

"Well, there's plenty more where that came from, so eat up. It stopped snowing," she said as she poured coffee in Jenny's cup. "Is Cord up?"

"Mmm," Jenny swallowed and took a drink of the strong coffee before answering. "I think I heard him in the bathroom when I came down." She sipped more coffee to cover the lie.

"Good, good. The sheriff called and wants to talk to him. Doc should be here soon to see you, dear."

"Oh, you should call Doc Prescott back. There's no need bringing him into this mess when I'm feeling so much better. I'm sure it was just a virus."

"I'll be the judge of that, young lady. Hope you don't mind, Estelee," the portly, white-haired gentleman came into the kitchen and went straight to Miss Estelee to plant a kiss on her cheek, which reddened instantly. "I let myself in."

Miss Estelee brushed him off. "Of course I don't mind. Sit and I'll get you a plate."

"Thank you, dear," he said with a twinkle in his eye.

Jenny smiled. She'd always thought the town doctor looked a little like Santa.

"Jenny!" He came to her and kissed her cheek as well. "I can't tell you how glad I am to see you. It was quite a pleasant surprise to learn you'd risen from the dead."

Jenny set her cup aside. "Well, it wasn't quite that dramatic. Just a little misunderstanding."

"I should say that's quite an understatement, young lady."

"Truth is, I wish Grady hadn't told you that I'm here. I don't like pulling so many people into my troubles."

He sat and patted her hand. "Now don't

you worry yourself about that. I'm told you've been ill, and these scratches on your hands and face. They haven't been properly tended."

He made a clicking sound with his tongue. She touched her cheek with her hand. "These? They're nothing. And as for whatever it was I came down with after I got to town, I haven't had any symptoms for two days."

Miss Estelee set a plate and coffee in front of him. "Thank you, dear," he said. To Jenny, he asked, "And the symptoms were?"

"Fever, congestion, nausea, and she was lethargic. She also had an allergic reaction to aspirin," Cord supplied as he came into the room.

"And you are?" the doctor asked.

"Cord Goins, sir. I've been with Jenny since the marshals lost her up on the Laurel Mountain."

Doc Prescott stood, and the two men shook hands — took each other's measure. "I do hope it was a good thing that you found her."

"Yes, sir," Cord said, holding the man's hand in a firm grip.

"It must have been something viral," Jenny added.

After a moment, the doctor released his

hand. "Possibly, but I'll still want to examine you."

"No debates so early in the morning," Miss Estelee interjected as she set another plate of food and coffee on the table for Cord. "I won't have anyone getting indigestion over this fine meal."

"Agreed." Jenny lifted her coffee mug.

"Cord, you look a might different this morning."

He stroked his face and looked at Jenny. "Thought I'd shave. I used a razor and shave cream you had upstairs. I hope you don't mind."

"Of course not. What do you think, Jenny?"

"I think he looks very handsome, with or without the beard."

Miss Estelee and Doc Prescott exchanged looks, but didn't comment. They finished breakfast, and then Jenny and the doctor retired to Miss Estelee's sitting room, opposite the more formal parlor. After a thorough examination, he put cream and bandages on her hands and declared her "fit as a fiddle," but that he would want to do blood work. He'd come by tomorrow morning to take it before she had breakfast. The scrape on her face, he just put ointment on. "It's very important to keep this moist so it won't scar. Apply this cream three times a day."

"Thank you, Doc."

They emerged to find the sheriff and a man she'd never met talking to Cord in the parlor. He was tall with short blond hair and wore a suit and tie. "Well, you'll all be happy to know, I'm in perfect health," Jenny announced. The men stood as they entered the room.

"She needs some fattening up, and I want to do some blood work before I have the final say on the matter."

"I'll see that she eats," Miss Estelee said.

Her eyes skidded to Cord's, then away. Taking in the other two men in the room, she figured they'd been having a serious and unpleasant conversation.

"Jenny," Grady said, "this is Jay Kennedy. He's with the Tennessee Bureau of Investigation. He's the liaison between you and the Attorney General."

Jenny shook the man's hand. "Mr. Kennedy."

"Please, call me Jay." He gestured toward the couch. "Let's sit."

"I'll take my leave then," Doc Prescott said. "Estelee, will you see me out?"

"Yes, yes. And then I have a cake in the oven that needs checking."

Jenny laughed. "Guess I know how to clear a room, huh?"

Jay spoke first. "I just want to tell you how sorry I am that your safety has been so precarious since you were taken into custody. I can assure you that won't be an issue from here on out. You're in the best of hands now, and the Grand Jury will convene tomorrow so that the evidence you gave to us can be presented."

That took Jenny off guard. "How can the Grand Jury convene in this weather? Aren't the roads closed?"

"Yes, but emergency responders are picking them up and bringing them into Greeneville."

"Wow."

"We have a video conference call scheduled between you and the AG handling the case this afternoon. We've set up the equipment at the sheriff's office. So, we'll be transferring you this afternoon for that."

"And the purpose for the conference call?"

"She would like to go over the evidence with you."

"She wants to go over my testimony, then?"

"No. You won't be testifying."

"What?" she and Grady said at the same time.

"Your testimony isn't necessary. The evidence you uncovered stands alone. The AG believes she can present it to the Grand Jury and get the indictments needed handed down."

Jenny digested that piece of information, astonished. "So, why am I in witness protection if I won't be testifying?"

Grady spoke up. "Because the crime ring knows that you uncovered the information and turned it over to authorities."

"So did you."

"You're seen as the target. My involvement wasn't apparent. I was simply seen as the guy making arrests."

"This is crazy."

"The silver lining in all this, if there is one, is that we'll be able to move up your relocation."

She did look at Cord then. He was leaning forward, staring at his linked hands. She turned back to Jay. "When?" Her voice cracked as she said the word.

"As soon as tomorrow, if all goes as expected with the Grand Jury."

Tomorrow? Dear Lord, the space she'd seen so clearly just last night, the space she and Cord had shared, disappeared with that single word.

"I know you've been through a lot, but

it's almost over," Jay said. "You are my priority. I will personally oversee your placement. There will be no more, *um,* precarious predicaments for you to navigate."

She knew she should say something like *thank you,* but at this moment, immediate relocation was the last thing she could consider. After all this time and all she'd been through, now? How could it come now?

"Where am I going?"

"You'll be given the information when we're en route."

"Who will know where I am besides you?" She looked at Cord, then back. "Grady?"

"No one," Jay said.

Panic bubbled up inside her. Her body felt about to shatter, her soul began a slow fracture splitting her right down the middle. She looked at Cord again. How could he just quietly sit there? She stood. "If that's all for now, I — I —"

"Of course. We'll come get you a bit before two," Jay said. "Grady, I believe we have some prisoners to deal with?"

"Yes."

The two men showed themselves out, leaving Jenny alone with Cord in the parlor.

"Are you all right?" he asked.

Jenny walked over to the curio cabinet

filled with angels. She couldn't breathe. She wasn't ready for this. She had to get out of here.

"I'm not feeling well. I think I need to lie down." She turned to walk out of the room and go upstairs without looking at Cord, but he was there beside her, grasping her arm.

"I'll take you up."

"No." She tried to look at him, but the pain surged strong and raw, and she couldn't. "I need to be alone."

He let her go and she ran up the stairs.

"Well what are you waitin' on, young man?"

Miss Estelee had appeared before him without his noticing. A door closed above them. He sighed and hung his head.

Miss Estelee sighed as well. "You're right." Eyeing the stairway, she held out her hand. "Help me get up these, would you Cord?"

Instead of offering his hand, he lifted her into his arms and carried her up the stairs. "Well! I must say, it's been quite some years since a strapping young man —"

He deposited her carefully at the top of the stairs before she could finish her statement. She smoothed her skirt and simply said, "Thank you."

Cord nodded and went back downstairs.

Jenny didn't know how Miss Estelee got up the stairs or how she knew which room she was in, but when the older woman opened and closed her door, she was not happy for the intrusion. She swiped at tears with the back of her hand, wishing she could just disappear and pretend the last few months were a bad dream.

Miss Estelee sat next to her on the bed. "You've faced everything up to now head-on. What's holding you back now? I'd think you'd be happy to finally see an end in sight."

Jenny didn't know where to begin. All the months of running, hiding, being found, hidden and found again — she *should* be happy to see it all end. How could she say that's exactly what she didn't want? For it to end now? Miss Estelee had predicted she'd find the love of her life. She hadn't said she'd have to leave him behind.

"The Bible says that there is a season for everything. A time for beginnings and endings, a time to be happy and sad, a time to mourn and a time to dance. But as I see it, we spend most all our lives somewhere in the middle. Not starting or ending, not happy or sad, just being." She took Jenny's hand and held it in both of her old, bent ones. "It's what we do in those 'in between' states that makes up our living.

"Look over there, dear."

Jenny sniffed and looked up to see Miss Estelee point to the corner of the room.

"Do you see that spider web over by the window? Isn't it beautiful, glistening in the sunlight? So intricate and complicated. The hours and creativity that creature must have put into making such a wondrous thing. Can you imagine creating something so delicate that in an instant a wind or a careless hand could come and tear it down, just like that?"

She snapped her fingers, then quiet settled around them like a cloak. "That spider, she gets knocked down with her web, and she might spend a time mourning the loss of all she's worked for and the shelter that it provided her for a time. But by tomorrow, there'll be another web. Maybe not in the same spot, but another just as intricate and beautiful. Persistence and tremendous patience is wired into that spider. It's how she survives."

Jenny was sure that the woman was telling her the story to drive home some point, but her heart was too heavy to decipher the meaning.

"You've spent your whole life doing good, meaningful work. You've traveled your road, working alone like that spider over there, and you built a good life for yourself. But now, some senseless bandit has come and destroyed all your hard work." She rocked back and patted Jenny's hand again. "Look at me, honey."

Jenny swiped at her tears again, and met the woman's soft blue eyes. "Spiders don't have souls or the freewill to make choices. They just do what they were created to do. They don't know why they keep building those webs. They only know they must.

"God put them here for a reason. I believe it was so we could learn something from them. You've got a new life to begin. You have no choice in the matter. Now, you can go sit in the dark and mourn the loss of your old life, and no one would fault you for it. But after the beginning, there's that space in the middle where you'll have to choose. Are you going to just exist in that space, or are you going to create something intricate and beautiful there for yourself?"

"I don't think I have it in me, Miss Estelee."

"Honey, you got more strength in you than you can imagine. And if that strength fails you, God will give you His if you ask Him. He'll even send his angels to carry you, if need be."

She stood. "Now, there's a young man downstairs with a face longer than yours. I'll send him up so the two of you can talk. You've come to an ending, but you *both* must now begin anew."

The space she and Cord shared was closing. He'd built a web of protection around her. It had been beautiful but delicate, and Jay Kennedy would be the agent to tear it down. A new life stretched out in front of her, away from everything familiar and unlike anything she'd ever known. She couldn't imagine it.

When Cord walked in, she knew she'd be leaving her heart here with him. She stood and walked into his arms. This was home and safety and peace. Together, they were so strong. How could she leave this when she'd only just found it?

"I know," he said as if he'd read her thoughts.

She leaned back and looked at him. "I was actually hoping that you'd say something more along the lines of 'let's just run away together'."

He took her hands. "I wish that were an option."

"Sounds like a viable plan to me. We can relocate ourselves somewhere that no one can find us. You've already done it once.

You could do it again."

"Jenny . . ."

She took a step back and looked at him, really looked at him through her well-trained critical eye. Something wasn't right.

"You're an ex-cop. I figured that out right away. But there's more isn't there?"

"Yes." He looked everywhere but at her.

"Tell me."

He sat on the bed. "I don't know where to start."

"Just say it, Cord."

"My name isn't Cord, and I can't relocate with you because —"

He broke off then and raked a hand through his hair.

She took a step back and braced herself. "Because?"

"Because I've already been relocated. I'm in the program, too."

CHAPTER 18

"Never let it be said that a little bit of snow would keep the residents of Angel Ridge from turning up at my door expecting to be fed."

"A foot of snow doesn't qualify as a 'little' snow," Dixie's brother, Blake, said. "And we have Cole and Bud DeFoe to thank for cleaning the sidewalks, or no one would have ventured out. I'm sure a lot of people are glad you're open. I bet there were plenty of people who weren't able to lay in supplies before the storm hit."

"I'll be open as long as I have food," Dixie said as she poured Frannie Thompson a cup of coffee. "I'd imagine I won't get another delivery for a few days. So, I'm afraid the selection is limited to the special. I hope you like homemade vegetable soup and grilled cheese sandwiches."

"I'll just have coffee," Frannie rasped.

"If you don't mind me sayin', you look a

little green around the gills. Are you under the weather, hon?"

"Didn't sleep well last night," she explained without looking up from her coffee.

"Well, that's not surprising given that you're staying at Jenny's house for the first time."

"Thank you for the coffee," Frannie said between sips.

Patrick Houston and Grady came in with a frigid wind blowing through the open door. "Get in here and close the door," Dixie said. "It's colder'n a witch's you-know-whats out there." She set two more mugs on the lunch counter and poured, then took in a disheveled Patrick with dark circles and bloodshot eyes. "Good Lord, Patrick. What happened to you?"

"Didn't sleep well last night," he grumbled.

Jenny's sister did look up then, but quickly turned away.

Dixie frowned. "Seems to be goin' around. You boys havin' lunch?"

"Yeah, and I'm kinda in a hurry. It's crazy at the station," Grady said. "Can I just get two specials to go?"

"We didn't finish our conversation last night, Grady, and don't think I've forgotten it."

"I'm sorry, Dix. I just don't have time to go into it right now."

"*Uh-huh.* How 'bout you, Patrick?"

"Just coffee."

"Glad to see you, Miss Thompson," Grady said. "I haven't forgotten about meeting with you either. I'm sorry I've been so out of pocket. I won't be free today until four. Will that work for you?"

Frannie nodded, but never quite looked at him. Dixie frowned. Something was not right here. And then Patrick confirmed her suspicions by saying, "Dixie, I'll just take that coffee to go. I forgot, but I have an appointment."

"Really?" She filled a paper cup with coffee, put a lid on it and handed it to him. "In this weather?"

He put a dollar on the counter and slid on sunglasses before heading back outside, but not before he chanced a sideways look at Jenny Thompson's sister.

"What's with him?" Dixie wondered aloud.

"Cut him some slack, Dix. He's got a lot on his plate," Blake said as he filled bowls with soup and set them on the counter in front of the waiting customers.

"Oh right, poor Patrick," Dixie replied sarcastically. "He's not the one with cancer;

his wife, who I'm sure you remember is my best friend as well as the finest woman I've ever known, is the one with the real struggle."

"They're both going through it, Sis," Blake said softly.

"Whatever. Can I get you anything else?" she asked Frannie.

"Is there a bathroom?" Frannie asked.

"It's in the back."

The woman bolted just as Bud Defoe from the hardware store burst into the diner. "Sheriff! There's trouble over to the hardware. You best come."

"Calm down, Bud. What is it?"

"Some kids were sleddin' down the hill on Lover's Lane, and little Sam Houston's gone and fallen into a hole! We need help. Somebody should go for Doc."

"Sammie's daddy just left," Dixie said.

"I caught him. He's on his way over there now."

"Blake, I have to —"

"Go."

Dixie took off her apron and was the first to the door, grabbing her coat and shrugging into it as she set off across Town Square at a run.

"What do you mean she's gone?" Jay

277

shouted at Cord.

"She's gone," Cord repeated. He still wasn't sure how it had happened. As soon as he'd told Jenny the truth, she'd rushed out of the room. He followed, but couldn't find her anywhere. He figured she had gone into the bathroom since the door was closed. Thinking she needed some privacy, he'd waited. But after fifteen minutes had passed, he knocked on the door, repeatedly. When he got no response, he opened it, found it vacant and the window open. He still couldn't believe she'd climbed down from the second floor. "I came here to tell the sheriff before doing a more thorough search. She has to be in town somewhere."

Kennedy grabbed his coat and punched some numbers into his cell. "Sheriff, our package has disappeared." To Cord he asked, "How long?"

"About an hour."

Kennedy relayed the information and then added, "Right. Meet you there."

Cord tried to follow, but Jay rounded on him. "Where do you think you're going?"

"To find Jenny."

"The last thing I need is two protected witnesses exposing themselves to the general populace."

"I can't just stay here and do nothing!"

"If you want to keep her safe, that's exactly what you'll do. Of all people, you should understand the dangers." He shrugged into his coat. "Stay here. I'll deal with you later."

Cord bided his time, then when everyone returned to their business, left out the back way.

A crowd had gathered at the opposite end of Main Street. Afraid that the townspeople had found Jenny, Cord sprinted until he reached the group. He had visions of people mobbing her, happy or upset to find her alive after all, and asking all manner of questions. He did find her in the midst of a crowd of onlookers, dwarfed and thankfully concealed by his coat, crouching over a screaming toddler with bright red curls and a healthy supply of freckles.

"What's going on?" Cord asked someone.

Jenny turned at the sound of his voice, but didn't reveal her face from beneath the hood of his coat. A woman he recognized as the cashier from the hardware store said, "Little Sammie Houston came flying down the hill on his sled, got sideways, rolled halfway down, then wandered over to the hardware store's parking lot, kinda like he was disoriented, and went and got his foot caught in a storm drain."

Jenny spoke softly into the boy's ear and smoothed his tousled curls with one hand while she loosened the laces on his sneaker with the other. Miraculously, the boy quieted and nodded his head in response. In the next instant, he wriggled his trapped foot out of his sneaker and displayed a dirty sock to his audience. With a big grin he declared, "Not stuck no more!"

Jenny spoke again into the boy's ear. He wiggled his toes and rotated his ankle demonstrating that everything was fine. She helped the little boy to his feet, and he immediately bent at the waist, pressing his face to the drain. He stood back up with a forlorn look on his face. "Shoe gone," he said, then burst into tears.

A thin, pale woman, who must have been the boy's mother, appeared at that point, grabbing the boy and hugging the breath out of him. A man joined them, lifted the boy and put his arm around the woman, holding her close. Cord grabbed Jenny's hand as she tried to fade into the background and hustled her into the alley behind the hardware store.

"What the hell?"

"Sammie was stuck and screaming bloody murder. I was the only one around, so I went to help him."

"So you just thought you'd walk into an exposed parking lot, where anyone could recognize you, and lend a hand? Are you crazy?"

"I was careful to make sure no one saw my face."

"Damn it, Jenny. That was an unnecessary risk! And I won't even mention you climbing out of a second-floor window. You must have come back inside to get my coat while I was waiting for you upstairs."

She started walking, probably intending to get away from him, but he grabbed her arm, stopping her progress. "Where do you think you're going?" Jenny tried to pull her arm out of his grip, but he didn't release her.

"Let me go."

Gritting his teeth, he pulled her, resisting, toward the sheriff's office just beyond the other end of the alley. "Wallace and Kennedy are out looking for you. You have an appointment at the sheriff's office, in case you forgot."

She dug in her heels and wrenched out of his grasp. "I'm not going!"

"Think about what you're saying, Jenny. After all that you've been through, you're going to let these guys get away with what they've done to your life and countless others? When they're released, they'll come after you even harder."

"Stop! I don't want to think about any of that. I'm sick of this controlling my life."

Jenny eased down the wall of the alley and sat in the snow with her head in her hands.

"Think of all the lives this crime ring will continue to ruin. They may even come back to Angel Ridge and finish what they started with your friend, Candi. You're endangering your life and the lives of anyone you come into contact with if you walk away."

She looked at him, a wild, tortured look in her eyes that shook his resolve.

"You should know. Who's after you? Who are you hiding from?"

"You know I can't discuss that."

She tried to stand, slipped on a patch of ice, caught herself and took a step towards him. "Right. You can know all the details of my situation, but I shouldn't expect to know anything about yours. I get it now — about twenty-four hours too late." She pulled her hood up. "I'll go to the police station, but I do not want to see you there."

"All right. I'll go back to Miss Estelee's and wait for you."

"No need."

"What are you saying?"

"I'm leaving tomorrow. No point in prolonging this, right?"

It felt like a knife had just pierced his heart, but in his gut, he knew she was right.

"Plus, you wouldn't want to endanger me or yourself further, would you?"

Her voice was cold, emotionless. What he felt at the thought of never seeing her again was far from emotionless. He wasn't ready to lose her.

He pulled her close and held on as she struggled. "Jenny, please. I don't want things to end like this — don't want you to leave angry with me."

When she stopped struggling, he pushed her hood back and touched her face. Her eyes had changed. The woman who had shaved him, who he'd made love to this morning, was already gone.

"It doesn't matter what we want. Choices are no longer part of our lives. This is the end."

"We have today," he said softly, wanting to kiss her, but unsure of how she'd respond.

"I'll be going over the evidence with attorneys all afternoon, and then mentally preparing to leave and enter the program."

He took a step back. "Right, you have enough without adding us to the mix."

"There is no 'us'." She looked at him as if he were nothing, then added, "I don't even know your name."

Jenny somehow managed to turn and walk away without looking back, even though everything in her screamed against it. At the end of the alley, she hesitated, her resolve wavering. A woman rushed by. If Jenny hadn't skidded to a stop, they would have collided.

"Excuse me," she said.

That voice. Jenny turned to her without thinking, and the two women's eyes locked. "Frannie," she breathed.

Jenny's sister wobbled on her feet and crumpled to the ground.

CHAPTER 19

"What happened?"

Cord was at her side. Jenny had taken Frannie into her arms and was rocking her gently as she pushed her dark hair back from her beautiful, pale face. "It's my sister. My sister." She still couldn't believe it.

"Jenny, go. I'll stay with her."

"I'm not leaving her like this!"

"You have to. She can't come to and see you."

"She's already seen me! That's why she passed out." What if she wasn't okay? Jenny patted her sister's cheek. She had to be all right.

"I can convince her she didn't see what she thought she did. Go."

"Jenny . . ." Frannie moaned as she clutched Jenny's coat. "Is it really you?"

"Go," Cord urged, but Jenny hugged her sister close.

"It is you." She frowned. "I don't understand. You're not supposed to be here."

Cord muttered an expletive. "We need to get you both off the street before you draw another crowd." He stood. "Help me get her up."

"Frannie, can you walk?"

Her sister nodded. Cord, or whatever his name was, took her sister's arm and helped her stand. When he offered Jenny his hand, she ignored it and stood on her own. She took Frannie's arm and said, "Let's go." She pulled up her hood, and together, they walked quickly to the rear of the sheriff's office.

Cord stopped her just inside the door. "Jenny, we need to talk."

"I can't do this now."

"When?"

Ignoring the question, she propelled her sister forward into an empty room off the back hallway. "Why don't you go discreetly tell someone I'm here?" she said from the doorway.

He looked at Frannie then back at her. "She shouldn't be here."

"Get Grady and tell Kennedy I'm here. I'll deal with my sister."

Cord stepped in close, too close. Her heart skidded and before she could find her resolve, he slid a hand to the back of her neck and kissed her — a gentle, but firm slide across her mouth that fanned the flames of the fire burning between them, reminding her that the feelings between them wouldn't disappear easily or quickly.

"Later," he promised and was gone, leaving her to grab the doorframe for support.

"Okay, we'll talk about him later. For now, I need you to explain. How can this be? When they told us you'd gone into witness protection, we were told you would never be able to return to Angel Ridge."

She turned and looked at Frannie, her little sister she thought she'd never see again. Three steps and they were in each other's arms. "I'll answer all your questions, but give me a second. I've missed you so much." She put her at arm's length and looked at her. "How are you? You look like you've lost weight."

"This hasn't been easy, Jenny, and I'm *mad* as hell knowing that you're alive but we can't be together."

"I know. I've missed you, too. Losing you has been the hardest thing." Tears filled her eyes. "It's just too much. I need you, Fran. When we had nothing else, we always had each other."

Tears spilled down Frannie's cheeks and she squeezed Jenny's hands. "I know."

"None of this makes any sense, Jenny. Why are you here? It can't be safe."

"I know. Listen, I'm not sure how much I can say. I don't want to make things worse for you."

"Worse?"

Jenny shook her head. "I know it makes no sense, but you need to know that your being here with me right now is not a good thing. It isn't safe for you or anyone to be near me."

"They're supposed to be keeping you safe. That's why you went into the program, and yet you're out wandering the streets in Angel Ridge alone. I don't get it."

She looked away, but knew her sister would read her like she always had. "All I can say is that things haven't gone as they should."

"Jenny," Grady came into the room without knocking, "this is a witch's cauldron if ever I've seen one." He paused when he saw Frannie in the room. "Ms. Thompson, you're the last person I expected to find here."

"Sorry to disappoint," Frannie said, clearly angry now. She stood, arms crossed, and faced Grady.

Jay Kennedy came into the room, but

pulled up short. "Who's this?" he asked Jenny.

"My sister."

"What have you told her?"

"Nothing."

"Good."

"Excuse me," Frannie said, "but if you think I'm going to leave this room without a full explanation as to what's going on here, you are sadly mistaken."

"You'll do as you're told," Jay said softly.

"And who are you?"

The tall, blond man stepped forward, hand extended. "Jay Kennedy, special agent-in-charge, Tennessee Bureau of Investigation."

Frannie ignored the proffered hand. "That says a lot. From all I've seen, no one seems to be in charge of this circus."

"I couldn't agree more," Cord said as he walked in, taking up much of the remaining space and all of the room's oxygen as far as Jenny was concerned. Frannie noticed the change in her immediately.

"Honey, are you all right? All of you men need to step back! Give her room to breathe."

"I'm all right, Frannie."

"All the color just drained from your face."

"Why don't we all take a breath," Grady

suggested. "Let's sit and talk, noting that we are all going to act like professionals," he warned.

Everyone took a seat around the small table except for Cord, who stood in the corner of the room, ever near the door, a dark expression on his face.

Frannie spoke first. "Who would like to tell me what is going on here?"

"It is indeed unfortunate that you happened onto your sister, Ms. Thompson," Jay said to Frannie.

"And you thought that no one would? With her living in Angel Ridge all this time?"

Jenny started to speak, but stopped herself, unsure of how this was going to go. Would these people try to kill Frannie to get to her, even though Frannie wouldn't know where she was being relocated? The more she thought, the worse the possible scenarios became in her mind. Jenny linked her fingers and rested her forehead in her hands.

"She hasn't been here," Jay said. "She has been in a number of other locations."

"Why is she here now?"

"A series of poor choices on the part of the Marshal Service and the weather brought her here."

"She has to be in more danger in Angel Ridge."

"Yes."

"Who are these people?" She looked at her sister. "Jenny, what did you uncover?"

Before Jenny could answer, Kennedy said, "We can't discuss the details of the case without exposing you to the same danger."

"Will she be permanently relocated soon?"

"Yes. We expect the evidence she uncovered to be presented to the Grand Jury tomorrow."

"Mr. Kennedy," Jenny said, "what will happen to my sister now that she's seen me?"

"That all depends on your sister." He linked his hands and rested them on the table. "Can you keep this information confidential? Can you promise that when you leave this office you'll go on as if you never saw her?"

Jenny took her sister's hands. "Please, Frannie. I don't want you mixed up in this nightmare."

"It's a nightmare either way," Frannie whispered.

"These people are dangerous, Fran. You have no idea."

"But these clowns don't seem to be doing a very good job keeping you safe. It's dangerous for you to be here, snowed in. What if they find you?"

Jenny laughed. "It wouldn't be the first time they've found me."

"She has nine lives," Grady added.

"I don't find this at all amusing, Sheriff." Looking at Cord she added, "And how does this person fit into all this?"

"He's been staying with me for the past few days."

"He's some sort of officer, then?"

"No . . ."

Frannie sat back, a look of disbelief on her face. "Where are these marshals that are supposed to be protecting my sister?"

"I found it . . ." Jay searched for the right word, "necessary to take over your sister's care for the time being. Grady and I felt that Mr. Goins was the best person to see to her personal safety for the time being."

"How am I supposed to know that this isn't another in a long line of mistakes you've made, Mr. Kennedy."

"Excuse me?"

"What do you know about this person? Is he a police officer?"

"No."

"A deputy? An agent?"

"No," he admitted reluctantly.

"Then who is he to be given the care of

my sister?"

"Yes, Mr. Kennedy. Who exactly is he?" Jenny asked, her eyes never leaving Cord's.

When she at last swung her gaze to Jay Kennedy's, he returned her look's demand for complete disclosure, measure for measure. "Jenny, I can no more answer that question than I can your sister's regarding the circumstances that brought *you* here."

Right. He was a protected witness as well. Sharing the details of his case would endanger her in the same way the details of her case would endanger Frannie. But Cord now knew the details of her case, so what did that mean for Cord?

She had to admit, it was pretty ingenious. Placing him on a mountain, giving him the identity of a family member of a deceased couple who had lived on that mountain their entire lives. The story about him having Melungeon blood was a nice touch. He had the coloring to pull it off, too.

"I am sorry to cut this exchange short, but Jenny, I need you to come with me now. I have a file of evidence I need you to familiarize yourself with before we begin the video conference."

Jenny nodded and squeezed her sister's hand.

"I'm afraid I'll need you and your sister to

say your goodbyes now. The two of you can't be in the same location."

Jenny squeezed her sister's hand harder, not ready to give her up. "Can you set up a time for me to see her one last time before you relocate me?"

"It's not advisable."

"We're not asking you to do what's advisable," Frannie said. "I know the risks and accept them."

"With you in town, they'll be watching you more closely, hoping that you'll lead them to Jenny," Grady said.

"I understand."

"Frannie, I don't want you taking the risk," Jenny said. "If something happened to you —"

"Nothing will happen," Frannie said confidently. "Since Mr. Kennedy and the Sheriff believe they can keep you safe, I'm sure they can manage this small thing." To Jay she added, "So you'll set up a meeting between us?"

He exchanged looks with Grady, then sighed. "We'll do what we can. It all depends on the timing of the extraction."

"But —"

Jenny squeezed her sister's hand. "They'll do their best, Frannie. Won't you, Grady?" She gave Grady a long steady look. Finally,

Jay and Grady both nodded. She thought she saw Cord smile.

"Your mother and father must have had their hands full raising the two of you."

Jenny laughed. "You've got it all wrong, Grady. They raised us to be the women we are."

"And did a fine job," Grady confirmed, changing his tact.

Jay grumbled something about stubborn, difficult women before saying more clearly, "Jenny? Shall we?"

She hugged her sister. It was all she could do not to break down, thinking it could be the last time she would ever see her. She was the older sister and had to be strong enough for the both of them. There'd be more than enough years ahead to mourn the loss. When she at last released Frannie, she gave her a smile she hoped communicated that she would be fine. And then Jay led her into another small, windowless room to complete the final step in her journey before she would begin her new life.

"That went well," Jenny said to Jay and Grady several long hours later.

"Yes," Jay agreed. "Now we wait for the presentation of the evidence and the Grand Jury's decision."

"When will we know something?" Jenny asked.

Jay considered. "Depends on how long the jury takes to deliberate, but I wouldn't think it should take longer than a day."

"So, tomorrow or the next day."

"Yes."

"Have you decided on how you will move me?"

"Yes. You should be prepared to leave."

"Lucky for you I travel light these days. Will I stay with Miss Estelee again tonight?"

"I don't see any reason why you shouldn't," Grady said. "Your position hasn't been compromised."

"What about the men you arrested last night?"

"We questioned them individually, offered each a deal if they'd give up the location of others that might be coming in behind them. They wouldn't talk."

"Do you think there are more coming?"

"We can't be sure."

Jenny folded her arms. "But the roads are blocked, so we're fine."

"Absolutely," Kennedy assured.

"Weather's warming," Grady said. "Supposed to rain tomorrow."

That would cause more problems. If the roads began to thaw and people started venturing out, the people looking for her would have an easier time getting into town.

Another thing had been troubling her, so she asked, "Grady, how do you think they figured out I was at Cole's farm?"

Grady rubbed his jaw. "I'd like to think they just got lucky, but they've discovered your location too many times for it to be luck or coincidence."

"Do you think there's someone on the inside?" Jay asked.

"Someone in town?" Jenny's surprise made her voice rise. "Who —"

"I don't know. It's killing me to think it could be someone in the Sheriff's Office. I'd trust anyone here with my life — have trusted my life to these people."

"If it is someone in your office, Grady —"

"Right. I'll stay with her tonight, just to be safe."

"Good idea," Jay agreed.

"Will Cord, or whatever his name is, be staying at Miss Estelee's again?" Jenny asked.

"So you know," Jay said.

"He told me he was in WITSEC too, but nothing else."

"Again," Grady said, "no reason to do anything different. We need to be as low key as possible if we want to avoid arousing suspicion."

"You knew about him, didn't you?" Jenny said to Grady.

Grady looked away before answering. "Yes."

"Was he in the TBI with you?" she said to Kennedy.

Jay paused, then said, "That's not relevant. The important thing is Grady helped develop his new identity. They'll do the same for you in the place where you will live. No one will suspect a thing."

Jenny nodded. She could only hope that people as clever as Jay and Grady would be waiting for her when she arrived at her new home.

"Can we do anything for you, Jenny? To make this easier for you?" Grady asked.

Jenny stood. "I wish you could, Grady, but nothing about this is going to be easy."

CHAPTER 20

"Come in, come in," Miss Estelee said as Jenny entered the back door and walked into the kitchen. "You've had a long day. Sit, honey, and let me get you something to eat."

"I'm not really hungry, ma'am."

"Something to drink then?"

Jenny would give anything for a shot of whiskey.

"I know just what you need." The older lady walked over to an old-fashioned pie safe that sat along one of the walls of the roomy kitchen. She pulled out a dark brown bottle and returned to the table with it. "I keep a bit of rum, for cooking of course," she winked, "and for times like this."

Bless the old lady. She poured two fingers in a juice glass and slid it over to Jenny who downed it in one swallow. Her eyes watered and her throat burned as it went down, but she didn't care.

"Easy, there."

"Sorry." Jenny set the glass on the Formica table. Miss Estelee surprised her by pouring a bit more in the glass before she capped the bottle.

"No apologies necessary."

"Are we alone?" This time when she lifted her glass, she sipped.

"That young man's been prowlin' around here all afternoon. I don't mind saying watching him nearly drove me batty."

"Where is he now?"

"I'm not sure."

Jenny pinned Miss Estelee with a look.

"All right, I sent him out for milk."

Jenny took another sip. There was one thing she needed to know. "Miss Estelee, you said you knew Cord."

The woman stood and stirred something on the stove. "As I recall, I said I had seen him in town."

"No. You said you had known him before and after."

"I can't say as it really matters who he is. He kept you safe and showed you other, *um,* possibilities, I suppose you could say."

Maybe it was the liquor taking the edge off her raw emotions, but Jenny didn't react sharply to that remark. Instead, she said, "Please don't tell me *he* was the love of my life you predicted I'd find. If that's the case, I'm not sure I can face what's coming."

Miss Estelee pulled the glass across the table and out of Jenny's reach. "I have something to say to you, Jenny, and I want you to listen carefully and remember it when you get to wherever it is you're going."

When she was sure she had Jenny's full attention, she folded her hands on the table and continued.

"People enter our lives and leave. Sure, it can be painful when they go. A woman as old as me knows the truth of that." She tapped her chest with a crooked finger. "But as you grow older and experience that pain over and over, you come to understand that people who matter leave an imprint on your heart and become part of you. Though they may not be with you physically, they are a part of you. Their influence shapes you into the person you are. And in that way, they will be with you forever."

She got a faraway look in her eye. "All you have to do is look inside yourself to call them up, and they're right there with you to keep you company when you get lonely or times get hard."

Jenny bit her upper lip as tears sprang to her eyes. "How can it be the same?"

Miss Estelee leaned forward and covered her hand. "It ain't the same, honey, but the comfort in this sure knowledge makes life tolerable."

She nodded, tears misting her eyes as well, patted Jenny's hand and leaned back. She went to the stove. "Now then, let's get some food in that stomach. No tellin' when you'll have another home-cooked meal to warm you on a cold night like this."

Food was the last thing on Jenny's mind tonight, but she ate. When she looked at the empty plate before her, she couldn't have said what had been in it.

"Why don't you go rest yourself in the parlor? I've got a nice fire built in the stove, and I put out some books for you to look at. There's even a record in the phonograph if you want to listen to some music."

Jenny stood.

"I'll bring you a nice piece of cake once your supper's settled."

Listless, she wandered around the parlor. Not interested in reading, she stopped at the old-fashioned record player. Not sure how the thing worked, she turned a knob that got the record spinning then lifted the arm and set it on the end of the record farthest from the center. A scratching sound emitted from the speakers, and then smooth jazz piano, bass, and drums filled the room. Jenny settled into a nearby chair and, kicking off her shoes, curled her feet under her legs.

The next thing she knew, warm hands cradled her hand and warm lips caressed her knuckles, the back of her hand, her wrist. She opened her eyes. Cord. He'd knelt beside her chair. His dark hair had fallen forward hiding his expression from her.

He looked at her then, his eyes like black chips in his deep-set eyes. "Sorry. I didn't mean to wake you, but I couldn't resist touching you."

He kissed the inside of her wrist, her heart beating strong against his lips. The record had stopped playing. It was much darker in the room now, with only one lamp on in the corner.

"I must have been asleep for awhile."

"A few hours." He kissed her palm. "Can I get you anything? Do anything for you?"

She rolled her head to the side, still resting it against the high-back chair. "Tell me your real name."

He looked away then. "Jenny . . ."

She leaned forward and turned his face back to hers. "Tell me."

"Nicholas McCall."

"Nicholas." She tried it out to see how it felt on her tongue. It felt strange and out of place, like he had seemed to her when they first met on the side of the mountain.

"Nick."

She nodded. "Where are you from?"

"Somewhere in the Southern Appalachians."

She laughed. "So at least the part about you being from the mountains was true."

"I wish I could say I didn't like lying to you, but I never thought about it. You get so used to it after you've been in the program awhile, it becomes your reality."

"How long have you been in the program?"

"A little more than three years."

She looked away and chewed her lower lip. "Why do you live alone like you do?"

He shook his head. "That was my choice."

"Why?" She asked the question, but already knew the answer.

He stood and walked over to the record player. "I didn't want to endanger any more lives."

The sound of the jazz piano filled the room again. "So, what you told me about how you got your scars was true?"

"Yes."

The torture encapsulated in the sound of

that short, simple word tore at her heart. She tried to imagine knowing or caring about the victims who had suffered from the criminals she was helping put away. That would be so much worse.

"So, in the end, you got the bad guys? They went to jail?"

Cord nodded, still not looking at her.

She stood and walked over to him. "Do you dance, Nick?"

He didn't speak, but his arms closed around her, and he pulled her close. Jenny looped an arm around his shoulder, but pulled back. In the time they had left, she wanted to imprint the memory of his face on her heart, a picture to look at on the long nights to come. Surely it would take a hundred lifetimes to feel this way again.

"I'm sorry I reacted the way I did when you told me you were in the program," she said.

"You had a right to be upset."

"I wasn't upset that you were in the program. Not really. It's just this whole ordeal. It's all so unbearable."

He sighed and rested his forehead on hers. "Letting you go will be the hardest thing I've ever had to do."

"I've been thinking of all that time we were both right here, in and around Angel

Ridge, and didn't find each other."

"I wasn't exactly here. My cabin's forty-five minutes away."

"I saw you in town from time to time." She pressed her cheek to his. "A woman notices a dark mysterious stranger in such a small town when she's used to seeing the same faces day after day."

"I wish I could say I noticed you, but I tried not to make eye contact with anyone."

That gave her pause. "Is that how it'll be for me?"

"It doesn't have to be. I didn't want to invite questions; didn't want to form personal connections with anyone."

"That's only because you and I didn't cross paths."

"You do have a way about you that wears a person down," he said against her neck.

Jenny groaned when they heard someone knocking at the door. "What time is it?"

"Late." Cord was instantly alert and reaching for the gun at the back of his waistband. "Miss Estelee went to bed already."

"I don't think you'll need that. Guys with guns don't usually knock on doors. Besides, the door is never locked. If they intended to do us harm, they'd just come on in."

Cord positioned Jenny behind him, and

keeping close to the wall, opened the door to a closet near the foyer. "Get in."

Whoever was outside knocked again.

"Ask who it is," Jenny whispered, her hand on Cord's back.

"Who is it?" Cord said while unsuccessfully trying to guide her into the closet.

"Fuzz Rhoton."

"He works with the Grady. Remember? His property is behind Miss Estelee's."

"Right. I still want you to stay out of sight until I see what he wants."

Jenny held up her hands in surrender. "All right. I'll stay out of sight in the parlor. He's probably just checking to make sure everything's all right."

When she was out of sight, Cord opened the door.

"Hello. I'm Fuzz Rhoton. You must be Goins. The sheriff told me about you."

"That's right."

"Good to meet you."

Cord didn't return the sentiment. Jenny chewed on a fingernail. This was crazy. She'd known Fuzz for years. She was sure he knew what was going on. Grady had said he'd been helping out with securing the town after they brought her in. Strange though. He hadn't been with the men Grady had at Cole's farm.

"Mind if I come in?"

"Miss Estelee has already turned in, and I was about to do the same."

"The sheriff sent me over. He was going to come himself to stay with Jenny, but something came up and he sent me instead."

"The sheriff didn't say anything about staying here tonight."

Jenny stepped into the foyer. "Actually, he did, this afternoon after I'd finished teleconferencing with the Attorney General's Office."

"Hello, Jenny," Fuzz said as he stepped inside past Cord.

Cord backed up, keeping himself between her and Fuzz. "Hi, Fuzz." She rubbed her arms. "Someone shut the door. It's freezing outside!" she said with a smile, but neither man moved to do as she asked. An alarm went off inside her head. Fuzz seemed a little tense. The way Cord was acting was probably making him nervous. She shook her head and moved to close the door herself.

Cord grabbed her arm backing her into the parlor. "You should know better than to walk in front of an open door."

"Sorry! I'm sure there's no one out this time of night."

Fuzz chuckled and shut the door. "True.

We roll up the sidewalks at nine around here."

Jenny laughed. Cord was not amused.

"There's no need for you to be here, Rhoton. As you can see, everything is fine."

"Well, that's just it. There's been a change of plans. Kennedy sent me to pick up Jenny and bring her to the station."

The hair stood up on the back of Jenny's neck. "Why?"

"He's decided to relocate you tonight."

Jenny had to grab the back of a chair to keep from falling when her knees buckled.

Cord's eyes narrowed. "I thought you said Grady sent you to stay with Jenny tonight."

"Right. Well that was the plan, but then Kennedy wanted him to come get her to bring her back, but something came up, so Grady called me to come."

Jenny and Cord exchanged a brief look. Something wasn't right. She'd stake her life on it.

Cord pulled a cell phone out of his pocket. "I'll just give Grady a call."

Fuzz knocked the phone out of Cord's hand and delivered a kick to his midsection all in one move. Before she had time to process what was happening, Fuzz held her in a vice-grip in front of him with a gun to her head.

Cord had gone down on one knee, clutching his midsection willing his diaphragm to begin working so that he could breathe again.

"Fuzz, what are you doing? I don't understand," Jenny said. Dear Lord, he was the insider, the one who had been tipping off her location.

"I'd think it would be pretty clear for a smart lady like yourself. I'm not about to let you leave Angel Ridge alive."

"Why?"

"To keep you from testifying."

"It's too late," Cord said, on his feet now and moving toward them.

Fuzz cocked the pistol he held against her temple. "Don't come any closer."

Cord held up his hands and stood still.

"He's right. I turned the evidence over to the Attorney General's office and went over it with them today via teleconference. They're presenting it to the Grand Jury tomorrow. I won't be testifying. They have all they need to get the indictments."

"You're lying."

"It's the truth," Cord said.

"Like I'd believe anything you'd say."

"What's that supposed to mean?" Cord said, subtly moving closer.

"Indians, or is it Native Americans."

Oh Lord, Jenny thought. Fuzz was one of the crime syndicate. She closed her eyes and prayed — prayed to God and the angels that were supposed to protect Angel Ridge to save her and Cord.

"What in the world is going on?" Miss Estelee said. She shuffled into the foyer and then the parlor wearing her robe with pink curlers in her white hair.

"Keep back, Miss Estelee. I don't want to have to hurt you, but I will."

Ignoring that, Miss Estelee kept coming until she was so close that Jenny could smell the White Shoulders perfumed powder that the little old lady wore. Miss Estelee reached for the gun and said, "Give me that!"

Suddenly, Fuzz pointed the gun at Miss Estelee and pulled the trigger. Jenny screamed, but no shot fired. Just a click, like it had misfired or wasn't loaded. Then everything happened at once — Cord grabbed Fuzz's arm, Miss Estelee wrestled the gun from him, and Jenny brought her foot down hard on his instep. Fuzz yelped in pain as Cord pinned him to the floor, his arm wrenched behind his back.

"That gun was loaded!" he gritted out, his face pressed against the hardwoods.

"Guns don't work in this house, Fuzz Rhoton." Miss Estelee opened the chamber of the gun and emptied the bullets into her hand. Then she popped the barrel back into place with one hand. Jenny watched, amazed. The lady knew how to handle a gun. "This house is protected." She held the gun out and shook it at him.

"Miss Estelee, could you call the sheriff?"

"I already did. He should be here —"

Grady burst through the door, took in the scene and said, "Goins, what's happened here?"

"Give me your cuffs, and I'll be glad to explain."

Grady did as he said, but Jenny did the explaining. "It appears that you were right about someone on the inside tipping off my location."

"Fuzz?" he said incredulously.

"You have no idea who you're dealing with, Wallace. Trouble will rain down on you, all of you, for this. You may be able to arrest some of us, but you'll never take down everyone."

"What you've done all these years under the guise of a decent business owner in this town is despicable. It's the Devil's work that you've been about, Fuzz Rhoton!" Miss Estelee said, still waving Fuzz's gun at him.

"Here now, Miss Estelee," Grady said, taking the gun from her.

"It ain't loaded," she said, handing him the bullets. "Wouldn't work in my house even if it was."

Jenny's eyes were wide. "She's right. Fuzz pulled the trigger, and it didn't go off even though it was loaded."

Grady looked at the bullets in his hand and counted six. "Well, I'll be."

"Your mother's heart, God rest her soul, would be broken if she knew what you've become."

"I never cared what a woman thought about anything. My daddy was the one that initiated me into the organization. I wasn't the only one around here involved, either."

"But you're the last," Grady said. He hauled him to his feet and said, "Fuzz Rhoton, you're under arrest for attempted murder and kidnapping and probably a dozen or more other charges before it's all said and done. You have the right to remain silent . . ."

Grady finished reading Fuzz his rights as he walked him outside to his car to take him in to jail. Jenny sat heavily in the nearest chair. Cord was immediately at her side.

"Are you all right?" he examined her face, turning it from side to side, then checked the rest of her as well by running his hands down her arms.

"I'm fine," she assured. "Just a little shaken."

He took her hands and tried to rub some warmth back into them.

"Why don't I put on some water for tea?" Miss Estelee suggested.

"That sounds good," Jenny agreed. "Miss Estelee? How — why didn't that gun fire when Fuzz pulled the trigger?"

Miss Estelee cackled and clapped her hands, then pointed up. "The Lord works in mysterious ways. Yes, He does." She laughed and clapped all the way into the kitchen.

Jenny looked at Cord, shaking her head. "I told you things happen around here that can't be explained, but that's about the craziest thing I've ever witnessed."

"Agreed." He stood and pulled her up out of her chair and into his arms. With a hand at the back of her head and his lips against her temple, he said, "I lost a good twenty years of my life seeing him with that gun pressed to your head."

Jenny sighed into his embrace. "I lost a few years myself." She pulled back, touching his stomach. "Are you all right? He kicked you pretty hard. Is anything broken?"

"No. It was a cheap shot to knock the breath out of me. I'm fine."

Jenny sighed. "Will this nightmare ever end?"

"I hate to interrupt," Jay Kennedy said from the door to the parlor.

Jenny took a step back, but didn't break contact with Cord completely. She needed his strength until all of hers returned.

"Mr. Kennedy. I didn't hear you come in."

"Heard you had some excitement."

"Yes," Jenny said, sitting again. Cord stayed close as if he didn't trust anyone.

"If you don't mind me saying, I'm getting a little tired of having to apologize to you over and over for failing at seeing to your safety."

"You had no way of knowing."

"Nevertheless, it's time."

"Excuse me?"

"I'm extracting you tonight."

CHAPTER 21

All the breath left Jenny's body. She grasped her midsection and the arm of the chair. Cord squeezed her shoulder.

"Now?" she managed to say.

"Yes."

"But I don't understand. I thought it would be tomorrow at the earliest."

"Given what just happened, I think it's best to take you tonight. I don't want to risk anything else going wrong."

"It's okay," Cord said. "I'll come with you."

"I'm afraid that won't be possible," Jay said.

Cord took several menacing steps forward until he stood inches from Kennedy. "The hell it isn't. Try and stop me."

"Stand down, Goins. You know how this works. Jenny's safety is the primary concern. She's being relocated — tonight. I'm taking her into custody now, and she comes alone."

A few moments passed as his words settled on the room. "Take a moment and say your goodbyes."

Miss Estelee had joined them and said, "Mr. Kennedy, why don't you come with me to the kitchen for a cup of tea?"

When he showed no indication of moving, Jenny said, "Can we have some privacy?"

"I'm afraid not. I can't take any chances with the two of you leaving. My apologies to you, ma'am," he said to Miss Estelee.

Cord who had come to stand with her took a step back towards Jay, but Jenny grabbed his arm. "No. Let's don't waste what little time we have like this. Fighting with him won't change anything, and I don't want that to be my last memory of you."

He turned to her then, squeezing her arms before pulling her close. Jenny held on for long moments, breathing in his scent, his strength. After some time had passed, she pulled back and looked up into his beautiful face, memorizing every feature.

"When all this began, I never would have imagined that I'd find someone like you in the middle of so much turmoil."

Cord cupped the side of her face and kissed her; a kiss filled with such desperation and pain. Hot tears spilled down Jenny's face. Despair became a palpable emotion, threatening to overtake her. Losing her sister had caused unbearable pain, but that pain was nothing compared to this. There were no words to soothe this hurt.

They were both breathing irregularly and clinging to each other when they broke the kiss. "What can I do?" he said, his words ragged, rough.

"Let me go."

"I'd give up anything to not have to do that."

"I know," Jenny whispered against his cheek, kissing every scar on his face, knowing that fresh ones were being torn into him as they were to her. "I'm not sorry that we found each other."

"It's time," Jay said.

Jenny tried to smile, but her face wouldn't do what her brain was telling it to. She touched his chest. His heart beat strong against her palm. Remembering Miss Estelee's words earlier, she said, "I'll always be a part of you."

She sighed. Looking at the raw emotion on his face, she knew what he was feeling, because she felt it too. She stepped away from him.

"Wait."

He removed the necklace he said he'd worn since he was a teenager. He kissed the center stone, then slipped the chain over her head. Holding the pendant between them, he said, "Wherever you are, a part of me, the best part if it still exists, will be there with you."

She slipped her arms around his neck, and hugged him again. Then she took a step back, and another. He held out a hand to her, but somehow, she found the courage to turn her back on the only man she'd ever loved and walk away.

Jenny left that night, angry and determined to take back control of her life by whatever means necessary. When she walked out Miss Estelee's door, it was as if someone, or if you believe the legends of Angel Ridge, a divine being, whispered in her ear. If even that was too fantastical an explanation, she imagined then that the spirit of all strong, southern women — those who had nurtured her and others — rose up inside her like a tidal wave.

In the words of one great southern heroine, *As God was her witness,* and in the words of Angel Ridge's greatest heroine, Dixie, *She'd be John Brown* if she was about to walk away from the man she loved without having the final say about it. She'd given up her career, the business she'd built from the ground up, her family and friends, but this was quite simply asking too much not only of her, but of him as well. They'd both lived through enough to last a person several lifetimes, and the expectation was that they should also give up their chance at a lifetime together?

During the drive with Jay Kennedy to the airport, she figured she had two options; to lock herself in the bathroom and escape out the window, never to be seen or heard from again, or to wait and come up with a more viable plan. Since she didn't get the chance to go in a bathroom, she decided on the latter.

She flew with Kennedy to her new home that night. On the plane, someone changed her hair color and hairstyle. They dressed her in a way she would never replicate. Seriously, did they think that relocation required a loss of one's sense of style as well?

Her new name would be Jennifer Reid — Jen for short. All pertinent identification was handed over to her, including educational credentials to support the position of journalism instructor at a small liberal arts college where she was to begin teaching in the fall. Since it was still winter, she'd have plenty of time to acclimate to her new surroundings and situation.

After two days, she was left alone to unpack and settle in to a small Victorian in the Queen Anne neighborhood of Seattle. In the time that it took for her to unpack boxes and decorate her new home, she also hatched a plan in complete disregard for the dire warnings to not attempt contacting anyone from her former life.

Jenny asked a neighbor if she could direct her to the local library, to which she drove in her new blue Prius, making only one stop. She applied for and was issued a library card and logged onto one of their computers. She set up an email address using the name of her sister's favorite stuffed animal from childhood. The message read:

Mr. Honey Bear, please call Lilly Rose.

That had been the name of their pet rabbit. And then she supplied the number of one of two disposable cell phones she purchased on the drive over to the library, bought a cup of coffee, made herself comfortable in the magazine section, and waited.

And waited and waited. It hadn't occurred to her that Frannie wouldn't call, but as evening approached, she considered that she might have to go home, even though the place where she now lived felt far from that, and come back tomorrow to try again.

Then the phone rang. She answered it right away.

"Hello?"

"Is it really you?" Frannie said.

"Yes. It's good to hear your voice, but we shouldn't stay on long. I need you to do something for me."

"Of course. Anything."

"Write down this number." Jenny read her the number of the other disposable cell phone she'd purchased, twice. "Do you have it?"

"Yes."

"I need you to get that number to Cord Goins."

"Do you have his address?"

"No. You'll have to do some investigative work to find him. He lives on Cove Mountain, near Angel Ridge. His place is pretty inaccessible."

"Does he have a phone?"

"I don't know."

"Email?"

"I don't know that either. But listen Frannie, you can't let anyone know about this, so be careful about how you go about asking questions. Be sure Grady Wallace doesn't suspect we've talked."

"Okay."

"Cord may be hard to trace. No one knows this, but he's a protected witness, too."

"You're kidding me? What did he get involved in?"

"I can't go into that."

"I don't understand. If he's a protected witness, too, then isn't it a double threat? You could both get caught in the crossfire of the people you're being protected from if they ever found either of you."

Leave it to Frannie to bring up the facts of the situation she'd chosen to ignore. Frannie had always been the cautious one. She'd been more the "don't look before you leap and deal with the consequences later" type.

"Jenny, what's this about? What could possibly cause you to need to contact him?"

She sighed. Might as well just say it. "I love him." And then she forged ahead before Frannie could talk her out of it. "After you contact him, send an email to me at the address you have to let me know when he plans to call. I won't have the phone on otherwise. It's too dangerous. I'll check that email address at noon your time daily. Do you have any questions?"

"I don't know, Jenny. It's one thing to not have you here with me. It's another thing to not have you at all."

"You worry too much, Frannie."

"And clearly you're not worried enough," she complained. "How've you been?"

"All right, I suppose. I'm keeping busy, settling in. I've been under the weather and sleeping a lot. I guess that's a good thing because I would have thought sleeping would be difficult under the circumstances. How are you? What are you doing?"

"I'm back at work, but my heart's not in it."

"Quit. Life's too uncertain to spend your life doing something you're not passionate about."

"I know, but it keeps me busy. I need that now more than ever, but I'm looking for something else."

"Good, good. Did you sell my house?"

"No. I'm going to keep it for now."

Jenny smiled, happy to know that tie to Angel Ridge was still there. Maybe someday, Frannie would decide to move there and start over doing something she really loved. "I'm glad. I need to go."

"Can I email you?"

She considered that for a moment. "Only if you use a computer that can't be tied to you."

"Is that what you're doing?"

"I have to go. I love you."

Jenny disconnected the call. On her way out of the library, she took the back off the phone, removed the battery and the SIM card. She dropped the phone in a garbage can, then went to the bathroom and flushed the card. The battery, she tucked into her purse.

For the next few weeks, she made going to the library part of her morning routine. She found other branches of the library and rotated between them, careful to use a different computer each time. It got harder and harder to get up in the mornings, and when she did, her stomach seemed to almost always be upset.

Frannie kept her updated on what she had done to track down Cord. She found that he had a post office box in Angel Ridge and sent him a letter asking him to email her at a dummy email address she'd set up. She expressed how important it was that he do this, but there was no telling how long it would be before he checked his mail. All the while, she cautioned Jenny against going through with getting in touch with Cord.

Stubbornly refusing to examine the possible negative ramifications of her actions, Jenny settled in for the wait. Spring came, chill and wet in the northwest, but other than the Smoky Mountain skyline she had loved to gaze at from her screened in porch in Angel Ridge, there wasn't a more beautiful place than the Pacific Northwest. There were steep cliffs dropping straight down to rocky beaches. On clear days, skies so blue that it made her eyes ache. And the snow-capped mountains . . . Rainer, Mount St. Helens, and Mt. Baker, breathtaking.

Tulips and crocuses came up around her patio, a surprising riot of color in the gray-green landscape. She touched her flat belly. Another surprise she'd found as a shock was the baby growing inside her. It was still hard to fathom that she'd hold their baby in her arms in the fall, but that sure knowledge comforted her in the dark hours of the lonely nights. It was like having a piece of Cord to keep her from losing her mind. *Dear Lord, please let him contact me soon.*

After another week passed, Jenny decided that she would tell Frannie to go to him, whatever it took. The waiting was simply unbearable. But that day when she checked email, Frannie told her she'd heard from Cord and that he would call in an hour.

Her fingers shook as she searched her purse for the phone she'd carried for so long. Dear God! Had she forgotten to get it off the charger before leaving the house?

Just then, her fingers wrapped around it. Dragging in a shaky breath, Jenny willed her heart rate to slow. She switched the phone on and waited.

That may have been the longest hour of her life. She stared at the phone's display, watching the minutes tick by until 10:59 turned to 11:00. If desire alone could make a phone ring, it would have done so. But three more minutes clicked by before it rang.

"Hello?"

"Do you know how dangerous this is?"

"Cord . . ." His voice rumbling across the line and in her ear was delicious, even if he was angry. "Thank God you called."

"I shouldn't have."

"It's safe. I'm using a disposable phone. I'll throw it away and flush the SIM card as soon as I hang up."

"Then hang up now."

"No! Please!"

"What's this about? Are you in trouble?"

She almost laughed out loud. He had no idea what he'd just said. "I'm safe, if that's what you mean."

"Then why take this risk?"

"I want you to meet me in Lakeview, Oregon. Before you say 'no', hear me out. I'm moving."

"WITSEC is moving you there?"

"No."

"You're leaving the program?" his voice rose as he said the words. "Have you lost your mind?"

"Yes, I am leaving the program."

"You can't —"

"I've made up my mind," she said firmly. When he didn't interrupt again, she added, "And I want you to live there with me. I want a life with you."

"Jenny —"

"I can't think of two more capable people than us. We can relocate ourselves, make it so no one ever finds us."

"What about your sister?"

"She won't know where I am. Frannie understands that she could lead the wrong people right to us. She wouldn't endanger us or herself that way." She took a deep breath, and continued. "I'm taking my life back. I'm hoping that you'll join me, but even if you don't, I'm going. I'm living life on my own terms. I can't live under this cloud of deception, knowing that I'm being watched and not knowing if the ones watching are assassins, or well-meaning agents or marshals who are just as likely to get me killed as keep me safe."

Silence filled the line, so she continued.

"I've already contacted WITSEC and told them I'm leaving the program. I'm driving to Oregon tomorrow. It'll take me a day to get there. I hope you'll come, but if you don't, I'm asking you to respect my decision. I've not told you exactly where I'll be, but there's a diner in Lakeview called 'Angie's'. I'll be there next week on Thursday morning. If you don't show, I'll understand. I won't come again."

"Jenny, please."

"I have to go. I love you."

She disconnected the call, disposed of the phone, and the next day, she left Seattle.

CHAPTER 22

Jenny walked to the coffee shop she frequented most mornings. There were a few customers, but not as many as normal. The cool Seattle rain must have kept people at home. She shook out her umbrella and left it by the door. Keeping her raincoat on to ward of the chill, she took her usual seat in the back, away from the windows that fronted the shop.

Kylie, the barista came right over to her table smiling cheerfully. Kylie was a college student who preferred afternoon classes, so she usually worked the early shift. "Morning, Jen! The usual?"

"I'm feeling adventurous today, Kylie. I think I'll have a mocha with a dash of cayenne pepper."

"All right then!"

"And a croissant with that warm chocolate drizzle. I'm really craving chocolate today."

"Well we can't have that. My grandmother

always said if pregnant ladies didn't eat what they were craving, it would mark their baby."

Jenny laughed. "She must have been from the south." It sounded just like something Miss Estelee would say.

"She was from Georgia. I'll have everything out to you in a second."

Jenny rested her chin in her hand and stared out at the misty landscape. Her other hand rested on her slightly rounded stomach. In the beginning, she'd felt really queasy and tired. Now, she was just starved all the time and emotional. The tears came without warning. There was nothing to do about it except let them come. And they had come often in the months since that phone call with Cord when she'd asked him to join her in Oregon.

Almost as soon as she'd disconnected that call, she'd known it was a mistake. All of it. She blamed it on her independent spirit and strong desire to control her life and everything that affected it. She'd been so angry when she was relocated she hadn't been thinking clearly. Plus there were her sister's constant letters reminding her of the possible dangers. And, of course, a baby changed everything. Her reckless leap before you look days had to come to an end.

She had another life to consider.

Her plan to move to a sparsely populated town in Oregon to live alone on the side of a mountain was not only completely impractical, but potentially dangerous. Impractical because she needed good, accessible healthcare for herself and her baby as well as a good school system for her child. Dangerous because if she were found, she'd have no way to defend herself or her child if the people looking to kill her came in a large group. She might be able to hold off one or two men intent on doing her harm, but what if a large band came? It didn't bear considering. She couldn't put herself or her child in that kind of jeopardy.

And then there was Cord. She'd be bringing him into her danger. She remembered asking him why he'd chosen to live alone, and him saying that he hadn't wanted to put anyone else in danger. She knew she had to do the same. She couldn't ask him to risk his life for her. He had said he'd been in the program for three years, long enough that his trail had gone cold; but not so with her, especially in Tennessee or anywhere else in the south for that matter.

He'd saved her life, and she'd wanted to be able to save his in return. In this way, she could do that. She'd rather know that he was safe on his mountain than watch him be injured, or worse, to be with her. At least she'd have their child to hold, love, and watch grow as a lasting reminder of the only man she'd ever given her heart to.

A tear escaped the corner of her eye, and she swiped it away. A man was sitting in the opposite corner of the café, staring out the window like her. He removed his ball cap, raked a hand through his dark hair, and then put it back on. Kylie brought her coffee and croissant, drawing her attention away from the other customer.

"Do you need anything else?"

Jenny smiled. "No. Thank you, Kylie."

"Sure. Just let me know if you need a refill."

She walked to the man Jenny had just been watching to refill his cup. Too intent on whatever he was focused on outside, he didn't look up or acknowledge the waitress. Jenny sipped her coffee. There was something about the set of his shoulders under his dark leather jacket that held her attention. She leaned over to get a better look. He was tall; his size overwhelmed the small table and wrought-iron chair. Though his dark hair wasn't long, it wasn't short either and looked to have the same silky texture as Cord's.

Looking away, she shook her napkin out and placed it in her lap. Everything reminded her of Cord. Why should today be any different? Bells tinkled as another customer entered. She looked up and the man turned as well. Their eyes locked. Her fork clattered against the table and onto the floor.

Kylie rushed over. "Here." She placed a clean fork on the table and picked up the one on the floor.

"I'm so sorry," Jenny mumbled.

"No worries. Hey, are you okay? All the color has drained out of your face? Are you feeling sick?"

Jenny cleared her throat, wishing the waitress would move out of the way so she could get a better look at the man. "No. I'm fine. Really," she insisted. She took a sip of coffee to prove her point and nearly choked on it when it didn't want to pass her constricted throat.

Frowning, Kylie nodded and went to wait on the new customer, who was standing at the counter and also blocking her view of — it couldn't be. Her eyes were playing tricks on her, that's all. Jenny closed her eyes and took a long, deep breath. Another sip of coffee, and she was feeling much less shaky.

And then the customer took his coffee to go and exited, leaving her a clear view of the man who was now openly looking her way. She couldn't see his brow or his eyes because of the cap, but the nose could be his. He had a beard, not as heavy as Cord's had been, more like a few days' growth. He was too far away for her to say for sure, but it didn't look like he had scars. The jaw was similar. And his lips — she pressed her napkin to her mouth just in time to suppress a moan of pure pain.

It's not him. No scars. It's not him, but the damage was done. A gaping hole had opened up where her heart used to be, and she wanted to fold into it.

She looked again. The man was facing her now. She grasped the medallion Cord had given her as if it could provide some protection from this demon that plagued her, making her think she was looking at Cord when that could not be possible.

He removed his cap, and his silky black hair fell on either side of his face to his chin. It was shorter. He'd cut it — no. It wasn't him. His face — the scars — all so similar, but different.

She stood and took a step in his direction, then sat back down. Impossible. No. It couldn't be Cord. She looked away, consid-

335

ering. She should leave. Just put some money on the table, walk out the door and go back to her house. That's what she should do, but she couldn't. She couldn't make herself move. Her legs simply would not work. So, she prepared to wait as long as it took. If it was Cord, he had seen her. Was still looking at her. If it was him, he would come over wouldn't he? Of course he would. If he wasn't sure it was her and left, then she'd know it either wasn't him or she'd made the right choice after all. For his safety, they should not be together.

He stood and walked slowly towards her. Dear God, it was him. He moved like Cord and his face was so similar, but the give-away was how he looked at her — with the same mix of powerful emotions as when she'd left him in Miss Estelee's parlor and walked out of his life to find her way alone in the world as a different person.

"Is this seat taken?" he asked softly.

She couldn't stop staring and certainly couldn't find her voice. So she motioned to the empty chair across from her, and he sat. He brushed his hair back again and put his cap on. Even though she wished he hadn't, she understood he probably didn't want anyone to recognize him. But why had he been sitting by the window? None of this made sense.

"I can't believe it's you," he said.

"Were you looking for me?"

He nodded. "Can't believe I found you. It's been two months since you didn't show at that diner."

"You went?"

"Did you think I wouldn't?"

"I couldn't be sure. You were so angry when we spoke." She paused, "I don't know what I was thinking." Now that he was here, she was at once elated and sorry that she'd ever contacted him. "I shouldn't have called you. Shouldn't have asked you to come to me." She pushed her food away and stared at the table instead of him.

"Are you all right?"

Jenny had expected his anger, but his concern threw her even more off-balance. "I'm well, if that's what you mean. Mentally and emotionally is another thing. I have good days and bad days."

"I'm sorry." He looked away, then back. "I expected you to look different, but seeing you, after all this time . . . it doesn't matter. You look wonderful."

She lifted a hand to her now shorter, light brown hair. "You don't like it."

"You're beautiful — radiant. The climate here must agree with you."

"Thank you." She looked at him, too. Really looked at him. "You look different, too. You cut your hair, you've lost weight, your scars have faded."

"I had some work done on them," he admitted, touching his face the way she longed to.

"Why?"

"I wanted to look different when I came to you."

"I'm so sorry, Cord. It was a mistake, my asking you to leave WITSEC and relocate with me." It would be so much harder to leave him this time, to walk away with his child growing inside her. Instinctively, she folded her arms across her stomach.

"I'm here now," he said simply, when nothing about their situations was simple.

"You should forget you saw me. Go home, Cord."

"I am home."

His tone was soft, even. How could he be so calm? And how the hell could he sit there and say things that made her soul come to life? Look at her like he'd never take his eyes off her again?

"Cord . . ."

"Why weren't you there? Did you send me to Oregon to throw me off your trail?"

"No. I had every intention of being there,

338

but then I decided I couldn't do it."

"But you didn't let me know you'd changed your mind."

"I didn't think I should risk calling you again, especially when I didn't even know if you would come."

He laughed then. He actually laughed! "What exactly is it about this scenario that you find amusing?"

"That you would think I wouldn't come. Darlin', I've been looking for you since you left Angel Ridge."

"What?"

"I knew it was an impossible task, but then you called. You actually had the nerve to call! And you found an ingenious way to do it, as well. You're amazing."

"Don't think you can veer off the subject by throwing pretty compliments my way. You were angry that I called. If you'd been looking for me all along, why didn't you tell me? You should have been glad I contacted you."

"I was glad. Your calling gave me something concrete to work with in finding your location. Even when you didn't come, at least I knew you were within a day's ride of that little town in southern Oregon. I got in a car and fanned out. I hit just about everywhere between Lakeview and here. I really hoped you weren't in Seattle. There are so many places you could be here, but I was prepared to stay as long as it took to find you."

"What made you pass through Portland?"

He shrugged. "A feeling."

"Now you sound like Miss Estelee."

He laughed. "I know."

"So, you've been out here since that day I asked you to meet me?"

"Yeah."

"What have you been doing? Showing people my picture?"

"Of course not."

"What then?"

"I've been harassing Jay Kennedy from the beginning, trying to get him to give up your location."

"I can imagine how that went."

"Right. I also wrote you letters, hoping I'd be able to get some hint from you."

"I didn't receive any letters."

"He wouldn't take them at first, and then he did, but he just mailed them right back to me. Said it was too dangerous for the two of us to communicate."

He reached in a pocket on the inside of his jacket and pulled out a stack of envelopes, tied with a piece of leather, and laid them on the table in front of her. Next, he reached in a pocket on the other side of his jacket and pulled out another stack, and then another from an outside pocket. There must have been fifty or more letters in front of her. In all the time they'd spent together before she'd been relocated, he hadn't said near as many words as were contained in all these letters.

She looked at all the letters, amazed, then back at him. "I don't know what to say," she breathed. Her throat closed around emotion bubbling up from deep inside her, and she knew the tears wouldn't be far behind.

"Then listen. I love you. I don't want to live a life without you in it, so please —" his voice broke, so he swallowed and then continued, "please don't ask me to do that. I'd rather die a thousand times than spend day after meaningless, endless day without you."

Jenny blinked to try to keep the tears from falling. Sensing her emotion at hearing his words, he reached across the small table and took her hands. "I know what you're thinking. I thought the same thing in the beginning. It's too dangerous for us to be together. I want to protect you from my situation and you want to protect me from yours, but we can move to Oregon or wherever you want. You won't be alone. I'll be there with you, to help you and protect you. Wherever we live, we can build a safe room in the house. If someone finds us, we can lock ourselves inside until help comes. I wouldn't take any chances with you, ever, I swear. I'll keep you safe. Just say you'll let me."

Hope bloomed, delicate and tenuous. All she had to do was say "yes," and she'd have what she'd dreamed of all these months while she'd felt hopeless and alone. Or she could say, "no." Tell him she didn't love him after all, and send him away. But oh, how she wanted to share a life with him, to raise their children together, and see their grand-children someday.

"What is it?" He tipped her chin up so she had to look into his eyes. "What's holding you back?"

"I convinced myself that I could have a life with you, then I realized it wasn't safe and that I would live alone, like you. And I was willing to do that because I thought it would be enough for me to know you were safe.

"But now you're here, and hearing you say it can work, that you can make sure that we're both safe . . ." she shook her head and looked down. "I'm afraid to hope again.

It was so hard," she looked back up, "imagining you there at that diner in Oregon while I was here, in my house, going crazy wanting to be there with you." She squeezed his hands. "That nearly killed me," she managed through clinched teeth. She would not cry because she knew if she began, she wouldn't be able to stop, and there'd be time for that later.

"Do you love me?"

Was he insane? "Of course I love you! Why do you think this is so agonizingly difficult? We can't leave the program, Cord. Neither of us can. It's the only way we can stay safe."

"So you didn't leave the program?"

Jenny shook her head. "No. Did you?"

"Not officially, but safe to say, I'm off the radar. Kennedy is going to be so pissed when I call and tell him what I've done."

"Why would you call him? Aren't you suggesting that we leave the program?"

"No. That was one point where I thought I'd have to convince you. What changed your mind about WITSEC?"

She looked away. "The program isn't perfect, but it's the best way to stay safe."

"You don't lie well."

She blinked, surprised.

"You never believed in the program. Never truly believed they could keep you safe after all you suffered at their hands before you were relocated."

She focused on their linked hands. "Things have been fine since I got here."

"I'm glad to hear it, but still, I have to believe something else caused your change of heart."

This was it. If she told him, she'd be inviting him into her life. Whether she agreed to be with him or not, he'd want to be part of his child's life. Either way, he deserved to know.

"There is something I haven't told you."

He released her hands and sat back as if he was bracing himself. "Is there someone else?"

"What? No! How could you say such a thing? I told you I'd never get involved with anyone and ask them to risk their life for me." She paused. "I just . . . had a weak moment with you."

"For the record, you're not asking me. I'm volunteering, gladly," he said with a huge smile lighting his handsome face. "So, what is this thing you haven't told me?"

She cleared her throat, but still couldn't get the words out. "I never imagined saying this to you, so I'm not sure how."

"You can tell me anything. It won't change how I feel, about you or the situation."

She laughed. "I think this might."

"Just say it."

Jenny took a deep breath and let it out. Still, she chewed on her lower lip. She didn't even know if he wanted children.

"Tell me," he squeezed her hand, encouraging her.

"I'm pregnant."

Cord's heart stopped, then thudded back into a rhythm triple what it had been before she spoke. His gaze slid from her beautiful face to her stomach, which he noticed she had covered protectively with her hand.

"I'm just beginning to show," she breathed, "but I haven't felt it move yet."

He stared at her, speechless.

"Say something."

No words came. He reached across the table. Placing his palm against her stomach, he eased it down, feeling the slight, firm outward curve. She placed her hands against the back of his, pressing it close. So much emotion flowed through him at that moment that he felt not just his hand shake, but his whole body vibrating with love for this beautiful, brave woman he didn't come close to deserving.

"A baby," he breathed. "Our baby."

She bit her lip and nodded, words failing her, too.

"What a miracle, that a new life would come from all this. That we could be together . . . you, me and our baby."

"You make it sound so simple. Like we're just two normal people starting a life together."

"It won't be simple. Nothing worthwhile ever is." He laughed. "Think of it. We could be a family."

"I haven't agreed yet."

He stood and came around the table to stand next to her. "That's my fault." He got down on one knee and took her hand. "I haven't properly proposed."

"Oh, no," Jenny laughed. "You really don't need to do that."

"Jenny Thompson —"

"That's not my name anymore. It's Jen Reid now."

"Will you do me the honor —"

"I always thought, if I ever decided to 'be' with someone, it would be something more along the lines of a civil union, because I'm just not the marrying —"

"Of being my wife."

When he said the words "my wife," something inside Jenny shifted. Physically shifted. A feeling of profound love and happiness washed over her that really was like something out of fairy tale.

"Your wife."

"My wife." He pulled a box from his jacket and opened it. Nestled against the velvet lining was a silver ring with a stone like the one in the center of the pendant he'd given her.

She touched the stone. "The place where all the elements come together," She looked up. "The joining of souls when two lives intersect and become one."

"You remember."

She caressed his face. "Of course I do."

He placed his hand on her stomach. "Do you remember the rest?"

"Life springs from the joining of two people."

Her smile lit every corner of his soul.

"Did you make it?" she asked.

He nodded, tears filling his eyes as he thought back to the night they'd created this precious life — the night they'd made space in the midst of all the chaos for each other. He'd worked on the ring all those months they'd been apart, dreaming of someday being able to give it to her and make her his wife. He'd never dreamed their child would be growing inside her when he proposed. "Say 'yes'."

She pushed the hat back off his head and let her fingers glide through his silky hair.

"Okay, but I insist on giving the baby my name."

"I hate to point this out, but 'Reid' isn't really your name, darlin'."

She touched the smoother, fading scars on his cheek and said, "Our baby will never know her or his heritage."

Cord placed the ring on her finger and kissed her. After several moments had passed, he said, "My child's mother is a fantastic writer. Someday, when she or he is old enough to understand, you can tell this child, and our other children, the story of us."

She eased her hands around his neck. "Children?"

He nodded, ridiculously happy.

"*The Story of Us* . . ." she said. "Catchy title. By the time I finish writing that book, it'll be long and filled with many rich, interesting stories."

He kissed her again. "And love. Always love."

Dixie's Farewell

"In the fall of that year, Abigail Frances Thompson-McCall Reid-Goins was born. Boy, that's a mouthful! That happy, healthy baby girl is loved and cherished by her parents every day. Jenny and Cord also cherish the love they found together in the midst of a terrible storm in their lives.

"Jenny runs a non-profit organization with a website where she is able to continue her work as an investigative reporter, working on cold cases. She has no byline on anything she publishes on the site, so none of it can be traced back to her. Cord helps her with the investigations and continues to make beautiful, unique jewelry.

"I cannot confirm or deny (I just love saying that) whether they stayed in Seattle or moved to Oregon or other parts unknown. As protected witnesses, for their safety and ours, we can never know where they are, but we can be sure that they are safe and secure and together forever.

"Just the thought of it makes me sigh. Not that I'm ready or willing to give up my independence for anyone, but I do sometimes wonder what it would be like to love and be loved liked that.

"Forgive me, but I guess it's the rash of weddings we've had around here in the past few years. All my good friends have found the loves of their lives and are living happily ever after. There's Jenny and Cord, and then, of course, there's Cole and Josie and my big brother, Blake, and the new lady doctor in town, Janice. Grady and Candi still aren't married, but they're definitely in love. Let's just say that their relationship is not what anyone around here would call 'traditional,' which fits Candi to a tee.

"And then there's the loss of my dear friend Susan, who lost her brave battle with cancer about a year after Blake and Janice married. With all that change, I suppose I'm feeling lonely and out of sorts. But with all this love blooming and babies being born, it reaffirms that love really does carve out that space that's new and stronger for the struggles we endure and survive.

"Things have been real calm around here since Jenny and Cord had to leave. Everyone has returned to a sense of normalcy, but we'll always remember that time when Candi Heart first came to town and showed us a different side to life in Angel Ridge. It makes us all more thankful for our peaceful little town where everyone knows their neighbor and lends a helping hand when one's needed.

"I hope you enjoyed your visit to Angel Ridge. Y'all come on back real soon."

DIXIE'S READERS GUIDE

1. Jenny Thompson, like me, is a transplant to Angel Ridge who was never quite welcomed with open arms by the general populace. Does this bother Jenny? Do you think she is confident enough in who she is and what she's doing to overlook the lack of the town's acceptance?

2. Cord is content to live alone in his mountain hideaway. Even when he makes his infrequent trips to Angel Ridge, he doesn't allow anyone to get to know him. Discuss Cord's reasons for these choices. Also discuss what it is about Jenny and her situation that draws him out of hiding.

3. Sheriff Grady Wallace seems to never consider there might be a mole in his office with connections to the dormant crime syndicate that Jenny uncovers with her investigation. Why do you think Grady

didn't consider this possibility? What are the implications of this critical oversight?

4. Frannie Thompson comes to Angel Ridge to begin to deal with the loss of her sister. Discuss the bond between the Thompson sisters and how the loss of their only sibling impacts the two emotionally.

5. Mayor Patrick Houston is dealing with the grave illness of his wife and my best friend, Susan. In a weak moment, he and Frannie Thompson find a brief escape from their pain in each other. I think it's clear how I feel, but please do discuss this moment in the novel and how this event influences how you feel about Patrick and Frannie.

6. Jenny and Cord fight their feelings for each other. Discuss the reasons why they do this. Is it because they wanted to protect each other, themselves, or both?

7. Miss Estelee continues to defy explanation. In *I'll Be There,* the villain points a gun at her and pulls the trigger, but the gun does not fire. Miss Estelee scolds saying guns won't work in her house. Discuss Miss Estelee and the role she plays in the Angel

Ridge novels. I could tell you my theory, but I don't want that to color your views. Where do you think the author is going with this character?

8. Jenny has an unflinching determination to right wrongs and expose evil. When faced with the choice to hide the evidence of the crime ring she uncovers or expose it and give up a life and family she loves, she turns the evidence over and goes into Witness Protection. I'd like to think I'd be so brave. How do you think a person, particularly a woman, finds the strength do what's right no matter the cost?

9. In Witness Protection, Jenny struggles with handing over control of her life. I for one, as an independent woman myself, can understand. Discuss how Jenny manages to maintain her independence and continue to make her own decisions about what will become her life.

10. Who are your favorite characters in the Angel Ridge series? Who would you like to learn more about and see have their own love story and why? If you care to share, send your thoughts to the author at Deborah@deborahgracestaley.com.

Deborah Grace Staley is available in person or via Skype to meet with your book group or speak to your group. To schedule an appearance, contact Dixie@deborahgrace staley.com

ACKNOWLEDGEMENTS

The author would like to acknowledge the Goddard College, Port Townsend, MFAW community whose love and encouragement gave me the courage to write again.

In particular, Paul Selig, Program Director, who allowed me the privilege of being part of this exceptional community, Victoria Nelson who saw something in me and held up a mirror so I could see it, too, Darrah Cloud who understood my vision for this book and helped me bring it to life, all the students in the program from 2009–2011, but especially for the Class of 2011 — You are, quite simply, Amazing!

ABOUT THE AUTHOR

Deborah Grace Staley is a lifelong resident of East Tennessee. Married to her college sweetheart, she lives in the Foothills of the Smoky Mountains in a circa 1867 farmhouse that has Angel's Wings in the gingerbread trim.

In addition to being an award-winning author, in her spare time, Deborah enjoys watching her son play college baseball and recently received a Master of Fine Arts degree in Creative Writing from Goddard College in Port Townsend, Washington. She now writes full-time and teaches.

Deborah loves to hear from readers. Please contact her at:

P.O. Box 672, Vonore TN 37885
or via her website at
www.deborahgracestaley.com.

The employees of Thorndike Press hope you have enjoyed this Large Print book. All our Thorndike, Wheeler, and Kennebec Large Print titles are designed for easy reading, and all our books are made to last. Other Thorndike Press Large Print books are available at your library, through selected bookstores, or directly from us.

For information about titles, please call:
 (800) 223-1244

or visit our Web site at:
 http://gale.cengage.com/thorndike

To share your comments, please write:
 Publisher
 Thorndike Press
 10 Water St., Suite 310
 Waterville, ME 04901